WILD WILD GHOST

MARGO BOND COLLINS

Wild Wild Ghost

by Margo Bond Collins

Published by Bathory Gate Press

DEDICATION

This book is dedicated to the memory of all those I have lost. My heart aches with the empty spots they left behind, but their love and support and belief in me echoes through my life and my work. I am forever thankful to have been part of their journeys.

WILD WILD GHOST

CHAPTER ONE

Ruby Silver gently reined in her horse at the end of Main Street in Rittersburg, Texas, taking a moment to scan the newly constructed buildings. Already, some of the wooden structures the German settlers had hastily erected were being faced with the sturdier limestone from the local quarry.

At least, they had been. The mild day boasted a bright blue sky with only a few clouds scudding across it, and a light breeze, perfect for the kind of heavy-duty work that the new construction would require. But no one was working. Not the sound of a single chisel rang out in the spring air.

"This might be worse than we expected," she murmured, then lifted her hat to run a hand across her face. Settling the worn Stetson back on her head, she swung a leg over to dismount, filling in the missing commentary—inserting words into the gaping blanks left behind in the running discussion that had filled her world for almost two years now.

If Flint had been there, he would have suggested a drink first, a way to check out the local landscape without stirring up too much trouble.

Not that he had been particularly cautious.

Not nearly cautious enough, in fact.

But he did like to get the lay of the land before setting out to conquer any new territory.

"Easier for a man," Ruby whispered.

You can do anything you set your mind to, she seemed to hear him say, his blue-gray eyes crinkling around the edges as they sparkled at her. *Smartest woman I ever met.*

She sighed. *So what am I doing in Nowhere, Texas in search of German ghosts?*

Right. Collecting a paycheck. Avoiding demons.

Remaining alive.

With Flint's death, she'd given up on actually living.

The side of a building offered some shelter from any prying eyes, and although she couldn't see them, Ruby felt certain that the denizens of Rittersburg—living and dead—were almost certainly watching her. Lakota followed her placidly, the intelligence in his own eyes half-hidden by drooping eyelids.

Reaching into the larger of her two saddlebags, she pulled out a wrinkled horsehair crinoline, stepped into it, and tied it around her waist. The dark blue and green calico skirt she smoothed over it had been packed more carefully, but it still showed signs of having been folded. Trading her leather jacket for the matching calico bolero covered the worst of the travel stains on the shirtwaist—but Ruby would never be mistaken for a lady in this outfit.

Still, at least she wouldn't be run out of town for dressing like a streetwalker. Or worse, for dressing like a man.

Again.

A smile crooked the corner of her mouth as she recalled the string of blue curses that had rolled from Flint over that incident as they rode away. "And then when you're done, feed 'em fish heads," he had finished. "After you saved their asses from a hellhound, too. Serve 'em right if you let it loose again."

But memories of Flint—even good ones, like this—always led to the church. That was the one place Ruby refused to revisit in her mind.

Ghosts.

She was here in Rittersburg to deal with some strange German ghosts. Real ghosts, not the kind that haunted her own memories and dreams.

Switching her hat out for a bonnet, Ruby shoved her blond hair up inside it. Little about the outfit was fashionable, but it was, at least, passably feminine.

Unless, of course, I am required to run.

Under that circumstance, she might have to drop the skirt and crinoline.

Again.

And it took such trouble to replace them—every seamstress she engaged insisted on attempting to require her to wear a corset.

As if I might be able to run in a corset. As if I'd want to.

Attempting to fight demons while wearing a corset? She would be dead ten times over.

Like Flint.

Shaking her head to dispel the thought, she rolled her shoulders back, stood up straight, and led Lakota back out into the center of the street, where the two of them took up a slow stroll.

Walking down the downtown avenue in the middle of the afternoon should not have sent a cold shiver up Ruby's spine. Nor should it have brought Lakota to attention, his ears perked up to catch any stray noise. The paint horse's eyes opened wide as he swiveled his head from side to side.

Having Flint's horse to warn her of impending danger wasn't as good as having Flint, but she found it comforting, nonetheless, especially with the half-finished buildings looming above her on either side. She watched for a flicker of life behind any of the windows, but the most she saw was a curtain swaying in the breeze.

This wasn't natural. She had been called in to take care of the town's ghost problem. As a Tremayne agent, she had the authority from the local bank manager, apparently also the town's acting mayor, to exorcise their supernatural problem.

Someone should have been here to meet me.

Stopping in the center of the road, she turned a wide circle, checking every possible angle—the tops of buildings, inside doors, through windows.

"Hello?" she called out. Her voice echoed back at her.

"This is creepy," she whispered to Lakota, using Flint's favorite new word—the one he had discovered not long before he died. "I don't think anyone's going to answer us."

When the answer came, then, it was a surprise—particularly as it came from all sides, and in the form of glass projectiles that smashed into the ground, landing around Ruby and Lakota and sending shards slicing through the air.

* * *

When the glass began flying around him, Trip ducked around the side of a building at the end of the street, pulling his horse Bandito behind him. Flattening his back against the wooden siding, he peered around the corner, watching the woman he had followed into town. She wrapped her arms around her own mount's head, tucking her forehead against the horse's and standing perfectly still, apparently hoping to avoid being hit with flying debris.

But after a moment, Trip began to notice a pattern in the movement of shattered glass. Instead of slamming into the woman, it first cut through the air past her and the palomino. Then, instead of scoring the buildings it should have hit at the end of its trajectory, the glass shards' paths curved in a circle around the woman and animal, until the broken pieces were swirling in a circle around them.

"What the hell?" Trip muttered under his breath, leaning farther out to get a better look. Realizing that all the broken glass flying past him had been swept up into the whirlwind of glass around the woman, he dropped Bandito's reigns. "Stay here," he instructed. The stallion rolled its eyes at him, but nickered. Trip didn't bother to tether the animal; his horse wasn't going anywhere without him.

If exploding glass didn't startle him, nothing would. For that matter, neither did various ilk of ghosts they had run across together. Bandito was steady, even if he had a tendency to bite strangers.

That thought brought Trip's attention back to the stranger in the middle of the street.

Was this woman really supposed to be his new partner? When he'd gotten the telegram from the Tremayne headquarters back in St. Louis, Trip had laughed aloud. He knew there were lady agents—he'd even worked with one a time or two—but they had all been stationed back east. No lone woman in her right mind would want to come out here to work.

Not when there were plenty of ghosts to be exorcised in civilized places.

Safer places.

I guess maybe this one's not in her right mind, then.

Might not be a bad idea to remember that.

He watched the glass-cyclone sweep up the dust around her, the cloud of dirt thickening until he didn't see the woman at all, and reconsidered.

If she can cause something like that to happen, maybe she's plenty safe out here, after all.

As Trip made his way toward her, the glass-and-dirt devil rose into the air. He stopped to watch it ascend. Then, with a noise like a crack of thunder, it was gone. Trip had the vague impression that it had sped away toward the wilds rather than merely disappearing into nothingness, but he couldn't have pointed to any particular evidence that made him think that.

Smoothing her hands down the sides of the painted horse's face, the woman murmured something soothing in a tone that made Trip realize he had been hearing her voice all along, a soft alto hum rising and falling under the whipping and tinkling sound of the glass tornado, somehow more noticeable now in its absence than it had been during the strange events on the street.

The horse huffed out a breath, and the woman laughed. The sound of it sent an odd shiver up Trip's back—not of anxiety, but of interest.

Don't be stupid, man. You haven't even seen her face yet.

And he couldn't tell anything about her body under that horror of a dress.

Reaching up, she untied the bonnet from under her chin and removed it to shake off the dust. A silken fall of blond hair cascaded out of it and down her back, and Trip stopped to stare, frozen by the glint of midday Texas sun off its golden sheen.

By the time he moved again, she had begun brushing dirt off her skirt in sharp, efficient motions.

"Ruby Silver?" he asked when he was close enough to speak without shouting.

As she spun around, it occurred to him belatedly that it might not be a good idea to sneak up on a woman who turned flying glass into a tornado and made it disappear.

Holding both hands up, he took a half-step back. "I'm Trip. Trip Austin," he said. When she didn't respond with anything more than a suspicious glare, he added, "Your new partner."

Her mouth tightened, her stare captured his, and she shook her head the tiniest bit—more a negation of the mere idea of a partner, he thought, than a rejection of his actual claim.

Trip knew he ought to say more, but from the moment her gaze had caught his, he had been rendered speechless. To be honest, he had expected someone harsh, sun-weathered and wind-beaten. Women out here were hard, and women alone doubly so, used to fending for themselves in a land that didn't reward softness.

Not that he would call this woman soft. Not exactly. Her mouth drew down in a tense, straight line and her blue eyes narrowed in a way that suggested she would eviscerate him if he took one wrong step.

But dang if she wasn't the loveliest thing he'd seen in a long time. The lines of her face looked as though they had been sculpted, like one of those fine statues he had seen a few times when he traveled outside his home country on Tremayne business, going to places other people considered better, just because they had more people. Because they were "civilized."

He suspected the west's lack of civilization drew Ruby Silver to it the same way it drew him. Deep in her gaze he detected a desolation that matched any desert landscape he had ever seen.

A man might die in those eyes.

But before he did, he would witness a harsh wonder like nothing else he had ever seen.

Perfect, now I'm waxing poetical. I haven't determined if this is Ruby Silver, and already I've got men dying from the mere look of her.

He shook his head, half-amused at his own flights of fancy.

"What do you mean, my partner?" she asked, and Trip had to think hard to recover the conversational thread.

"I'm with Tremayne Psychic Specters Investigations. I can show you my badge, if you'll allow." He waved his hand, still raised in the air, toward his gun belt without lowering it at all.

She nodded suspiciously, her own hand dropping to the gun belt she wore slung around the hips of her skirt.

As he pulled the Tremayne PSI Agency star in its leather case from its position near his waist, he admired the way her belt outlined those hips.

That's a fashion I could get used to.

The fingers that brushed Trip's as she took the badge were cool and dry. She examined the metal star for a long moment, then ran one fingertip across it in a complex pattern. Something mystical, probably. Some way to verify the badge's authenticity.

With a noncommittal noise, she handed it back to him.

They stared at one another for a long, silent moment. Somehow, Trip knew that speaking was the wrong way to go. Instead, he waited for her to nod so they might get started on their examination of the town.

Whatever had sent that glass flying in the first place was big and ugly, and the sooner they got to work tracking it down, the sooner they'd be rid of it.

Instead, Ruby Silver shook her head. "I'm afraid you've wasted your time," she said. "I work alone."

Without another word, she lifted her chin, spun on her heel, gathered her horse's reins, and headed toward the largest, most imposing building in town—the bank—leaving Trip standing in the dust behind her, not certain whether he should chase after her, or simply admire her as she walked away.

CHAPTER TWO

I hope he can't tell I'm trembling.

Ruby was fairly certain the skirt would hide the shaking of her legs, and leading Lakota should keep her hands busy enough.

Not that it should matter what he saw. She had expended quite a bit of energy—anyone would be unsteady afterwards.

Anyone but her, usually.

The cowboy had surprised her when he walked up behind her, and he should not have been able to do so. This had been the first time she had used her special skills since she had given up on reaching Flint after he passed to the other side, and it had taken more concentration than she expected.

Not for the first time, she briefly considered, then put aside, the question of her motivations for avoiding most of her supernatural abilities since Flint's death.

This time the use of her skills had been particularly draining, not merely from lack of practice, but also because she had encountered a competing force, blocking her own. Though far from the most powerful reaction she had encountered in her time, it had been stronger than most she had come upon in her days as a demon hunter.

Admittedly, she and Flint had not often focused on the human afterlife, choosing instead to concentrate their attention upon those malevolent forces that might more directly cause harm to the living.

"Broken glass on the wing might injure the unwary," she muttered aloud, much as she knew Flint would have, had she been able to have this conversation with him.

Hitching Lakota to one of the posts in front of the bank—all of which were otherwise unoccupied—Ruby took a moment to tidy her appearance, carefully tucking her hair back inside her bonnet and straightening her skirt. Should she meet anyone inside, it would not do to look unkempt.

Neat but plain.

She concentrated on the phrase, attempting to embody the concept.

It would be even better if she managed to look outright ugly. Grief had done its best in the last months to strip her of vitality, and that had actually made her first jobs with the Tremayne Agency simpler than she had feared.

But as she continued to choose life over death month after month, continued to eat on a relatively regular schedule, to sleep most nights, her natural vigor began to return to her, and she knew it would not be long before men began to take notice of her once again.

The thought caused her to glance over her shoulder at the man still standing in the street, watching her.

Having Flint around to deflect others' attention had been useful.

Then again, her former partner had been a mountain of a man, intimidating and prone to scowling at those he did not know. Few people had realized that the lines around his eyes were as much from smiles as from frowns or the glare of the Western sun.

Blowing out a sigh, she moved inside the bank, welcoming the cool dimness of the shaded interior.

* * *

Ruby considered casting another glance at the man in the street, but she didn't want him thinking about her watching him. Something about his aura bothered her, and she had to wrap her arms around her upper body to keep herself from peering back over her shoulder to examine it more closely.

It simply ... felt *wrong.*

Everything about this particular assignment had felt wrong since the moment she rode into town.

Since the moment she had taken the job, truth be told.

Since the moment Flint left me behind to explore the afterlife without me.

Tears welled up in her eyes and she blinked, hard, willing them back down to where they had been clogging her throat for the last month as she refused to let them out, tired of crying herself to sleep every night, alone.

She could almost hear Flint's voice. *Crying doesn't do any good, anyway. Everything will work out OK. It always does.*

At the back of the bank lobby, a short, portly, balding man in his late forties stood with his back against the tellers' cages, winding a pocket-watch as he waited for Ruby to make her way toward him.

When she was close enough for him to speak to her without his voice echoing through the marbled room, he said, "Miss Silver?" in a heavily German-accented voice.

Ruby nodded, but waited until she could respond without raising her voice. "I am. Mr. Schmidt? You contacted the Tremayne Agency for help?"

"Ja." He paused for a moment. "But you have seen the *poltergeist* now, yes?"

"I'm afraid I don't know that term." She kept her voice low and gentle. "I assume, however, that you mean the entity in the street?"

Mr. Schmidt nodded, then paused, searching for other words. "It is a ... you say entity? A *geist* ... ghost ... of .... disturbance. Loudness. Noise. Yes. Noise." He nodded, certain in his description.

"A noisy ghost?" Ruby glanced back toward the doorway and discovered that the other Tremayne agent had found his way inside, as well. She refrained from sighing, but only barely. "Yes, *noisy ghost* certainly describes what I saw outside."

Stepping close to Mr. Schmidt, she gently placed one hand on his forearm. He jerked away slightly. "If I may? I would like to see what, if anything, I can determine about the spirit you are facing."

Mr. Schmidt didn't try to pull away, but he was by no means comfortable.

That's going to make tracking down the source more difficult.

Everything was more difficult without Flint. Out of balance. When they had worked together, he had distracted the clients as Ruby had read them, learning how they remained connected to the spirits, how they kept the specters tethered to this world rather than allowing them to move on to the next.

Now, all of Mr. Schmidt's attention remained on Ruby.

The more he focused on her, the harder it was to follow the connections to the other side.

Nonetheless, she felt the tether. Drawing in a deep breath, traced the glowing white cord that tied Mr. Schmidt to ...

Not to one entity.

...but to many ...

What is this?

Ruby's concentration shattered into a hundred pieces. Clenching her teeth against the gasp that tried to escape, she focused on remaining still. Her eyes flew open, though, and she stared at the middle-aged man in front of her.

"Are you OK?" The Tremayne agent's voice was so close it startled her.

The term startled her, as well—it had been one of Flint's favorite slang words, its usage a habit of which she had attempted to break him.

A smile crossed her face.

As if Ruby had ever been able to break Flint of any habits he enjoyed.

"I am well," she responded coolly.

Turning to the town leader, he stuck out one hand in a friendly gesture. "Travis James Austin III," he said cheerfully. "Trip to my friends. I hope to call you one."

He sounded more like a snake-oil peddler than a

professional agent. Mr. Schmidt raised his eyebrows, but he took Trip's—Mr. Austin's—hand. As soon as he had done so, however, Austin dropped the overly-friendly act and began stalking around the bank lobby.

"A noisy ghost, you say?" He rested one hand on the butt of one pistol.

"Ja, but ..." the bank manager paused, turning to Ruby as if appealing for help, a frown crinkling his otherwise round face. "Pistols do not work against the dead."

"That is generally true." Turning only her head, she spoke over her shoulder to Austin, who had wandered behind her and was peering at a chip in a marble column, where apparently the apparition had taken out some of the stone. "Did you hear that, Mr. Austin? Your guns will be ineffective against the phantoms haunting this town."

If she had not been watching for it, she would have missed the flicker of his gaze toward her, the appreciative gleam in his eye. He frowned. "Indeed, Miss Silver? And are the good folk of Rittersburg certain of this? Have they, in fact, attempted to use my side arms against this disturbance?"

Clenching her teeth against a shout of laughter, Ruby widened her eyes and looked inquiringly at Mr. Schmidt, who stammered. "Of course not. That is, not Mr. Austin's weapons. But others, certainly."

"Hmm." Ruby nodded. "Yes, well. Please do keep in mind, Mr. Schmidt, that agents from the Tremayne Agency come not only well trained, but well armed. I am prepared to engage with the other side through a variety of methods, including capture, exorcism, and elimination, as is my co-agent." She didn't actually know if that was true. It was the spiel she and Flint had used when they had set out to convince a town or family to pay them to eliminate the monsters that had attached themselves to the unsuspecting.

The rest of the world had developed a love of the Wild West, with its untamed land and native peoples.

But Ruby knew that there were more horrors in the

West than the rest of the world realized.

Including the one that had killed her partner.

And someday, she would track it down, too, and send it straight back to Hell.

With a tiny shake of her head, she dispelled the thought. That day was not today, and until then, she had work to do—not least of all, learning to stay alive while she hunted down that demon, even without Flint at her side.

Still, if Mr. Austin had noticed her pause, he had ignored it. He was going over the Tremayne Agency's rules— all the things that agents were not allowed to do for clients.

For some reason, it bothered her, and she wasn't sure why. She and Flint had maintained a similar set of guidelines, even for the two of them, and she had never chafed against the strictures before.

In part, she suspected it was the fact that the Tremayne Agency felt the need to specify their stance against divorce. Not that Ruby was particularly opposed to divorce. She was, however, opposed to marriage.

At least for herself.

No. She suspected that her desire to rebel against the rules the Tremayne Agency set out had more to do with her unhappiness at going to work for a company at all.

"I'm no company man," Flint had said on more than one occasion. "Company starts telling you where to go, what to do, pretty soon you lose all sense of freedom. Next thing you know you'll be asking what to think. Someone starts telling me what to think, I might as well hang up my fiddle, stop hunting demons altogether."

Guess I learned more from his tutelage than I realized.

Ruby had also, however, realized when to remain silent. Now she began her own examination of the marble in the room.

Much more of the stone was chipped than she had first noticed.

This had not been the first ghostly whirlwind, then.

Nor the second, either.

The tellers' cages were also more fortified than she had initially anticipated.

This town had been under siege for longer than Mr. Schmidt had cared to acknowledge in his communiqués with Ruby's new bosses.

Pulling out a small sketchpad and a case of half-used charcoal pencils, Ruby began making notes of the placement of the chips in the marble.

When Mr. Austin wrapped up his conversation, he joined Ruby and peered over her shoulder to see what she was drawing. "Our host tells me there is something resembling a boarding house—a guest house with a beer-garden, I believe he said, if my ability to translate German is up to snuff—where we can wait until our rooms are ready."

"I won't stay in a brothel," Ruby replied without looking back at him. Not that Ruby and Flint hadn't stayed in worse, in their time.

Austin raised his hands as if warding off an attack. "I would not dare suggest it." He backed away. "I have a suggestion. You finish your examination of ..." he paused, gesturing in a circle around the lobby, "...this room. I will ensure that our quarters are available and appropriate."

Without bothering to ascertain if she agreed, Austin spun on his heel and marched out.

Ruby made a few more charcoal strokes on the paper, then leaned her forehead against the cool, smooth stone. "Oh, Flint," she whispered. "How can I do this without you?"

CHAPTER THREE

The new agent was an odd one. When the request had come through for his help training a new hire, Trip had expected someone green, an apprentice, not a gifted spiritualist. There were few enough legitimately talented diviners or psychics around, much less accomplished mediums.

"I'd lay odds she's a demonologist, as well," he muttered to himself as he made his way across the dusty street to the boarding house, the *Gasthof*, that Mr. Schmidt had pointed him toward—the guest house that was almost certainly also a brothel, though the bank manager had assured him he and Ruby Silver would be the only guests there this week.

So what was a woman like Miss Silver doing out here in the middle of nowhere, all alone? Back in St. Louis, she might have run an entire team. For all that the Tremayne PSI Agency maintained a veneer of respectability, all the agents themselves knew that the owner did not care if the agents were men or women.

For that matter, no one really knew if Nat Tremayne, the head honcho, was male or female.

"Or human, come to think of it." Trip was going to have to quit speaking aloud to himself, or that bad habit, combined with his unusual occupation, was going to get him strung up some day, put to death as one of the monsters himself.

The new agent now... she was definitely human. And all woman. His first glimpse of her hadn't been terribly promising, wrapped as she had been in far too many layers of clothing.

But for an instant, as she had walked away from him, the wind had lifted her skirt and revealed a glimpse of close-fitting trousers underneath. Hair the color and texture of corn-silk had floated out around her, and when she glanced back at him inside the bank, her eyes flashed a bright white-blue that matched the color of the lightning that had surrounded her outside.

With a grin, he picked up his pace, eager to begin to solve this latest mystery.

And maybe even learn why a talented medium had taken on a greenhorn ghost-hunter's job.

* * *

An hour later, he took a long swallow of what might be the best beer he had ever consumed. Technically, he wasn't supposed to consume alcohol on the job. But somehow he didn't think his German hosts would put *beer* into that category.

"Tell me, Mrs. Baumgartner, what is your secret?" He flashed his most charming smile at the round woman shaking her head at him as she wiped down the tables—but she didn't chase him off.

He should be able to glean some useful information, as long as the proprietress continued to view him as something of a charming rogue—certainly no one to take too seriously. "What secret?" she asked, standing far enough away that he could not wrap his arm around her waist, as he suspected many of her patrons tried to do. He had, however, winked at her.

"You are terrible," she had said, but she was laughing. "My husband is enormous. And when he returns home, he will crush you like *die Traube*."

"Then I reckon I had best make my move now." He raised an eyebrow.

Smoothing her hair down under a cap reminiscent of much European fashion, Mrs. Baumgartner practically giggled. "I have five lovely daughters, Mr. Austin, and many nieces who also live here. You should not attempt to court an old woman like me."

Trip threw his head back and laughed. "Somehow, I don't think they're actually your daughters and nieces, Mrs. Baumgartner."

"Indeed not." Ruby Silver's cool voice swirled around him—rather like being dunked into a cold horse-trough on a hot summer afternoon, both refreshing and shocking. "Nor," she continued, stepping down into the courtyard-style garden and nodding at the proprietress's offer to bring her a mug of beer, "would I exactly consider any interactions with those girls *courting*."

"It's not even flirting any longer," Trip muttered into his own mug.

"Pardon me?"

He would have sworn he had seen a flicker of amusement in her gaze as she glanced at him, but by the time one of the girls had brought a drink for her and thumped it down onto the wooden-plank table before her, the look was gone—and more than that, it was entirely belied by the expressions of concern she turned to the girls.

"Are you well treated here?" she asked one, placing a hand on the girl's arm.

"Ja," the girl laughed. "Frau Baumgartner ist sehr gut to us." Miss Silver peered deeply into the girl's eyes and glanced briefly around the small group of smiling, round, fresh-faced girls. She did not pursue the line of questioning. If they were in fact whores—and Trip was fairly certain they were, for all their language of family and "girls"—they were well fed, clean, and smiling the kinds of smiles that made it all the way to their eyes. He didn't think they were likely to be complaining.

Ruby Silver must have been satisfied with their appearance, as well, for she simply moved her mug of dark beer to a chair at the end of another trestle-table, set her sketch pad and charcoal pencil beside it, and swept her skirts to one side to sit down. She had changed her clothing since the events in the street, and he overheard her arrange in a murmur to have one of the girls remove her clothing and launder it.

Wonder if that includes the pants?

For a brief instant, he imagined her standing before him wearing nothing but the pants and tight, form-fitting shirt, while her gold-blond hair swirled out behind and around her.

Taking a drink to help wash away the image, Trip gathered his wits about him. He suspected he would need them to actually speak to this woman.

"What do you know about this town?" she asked as he moved to sit down across from her.

"Very little. Recent settlement, German immigrants." He glanced around the enclosed garden space. "Fairly closed to outsiders, though happy enough to take travelers' cash. Did the folks at the home office tell you anything more?"

A short, closed smile flitted across her face. "No. I was in St. Louis long enough to be hired, and then sent right back out. I didn't meet many people at the home office." Her expression suggested she would be perfectly happy to keep it that way.

"You?" she asked, taking a sip of her drink. Trip had half-expected her to push it aside in favor of something more ... he paused in the thought. Ladylike? That wasn't quite it. This woman wasn't soft. But she wasn't the kind of hardened plainswoman he had grown to expect out here, either. As a general rule, there wasn't much in between the rancher's soft, sweet daughter and his hard-bitten wife to be found out here on the frontier. Mrs. Baumgartner, for all her round smiles, was probably a more common type than someone like Ruby Silver.

And if that name isn't an alias, I'll eat my own hat.

"That's pretty much everything I know about Rittersburg," he said.

She flipped open the sketch pad and with one

forefinger, brushed and smudged a few lines before tapping at the remarkably good rendering of the bank's lobby. "This interior is still new, but the chips in the marble columns are either from several different events, or from one event that included attacks from a number of different angles." She turned a page and tapped the image, her voice dropping and becoming more contemplative. "I would need to take more precise measurements, but I would guess that this damage came from at least four different directions."

Trip blinked. "Measurements?" A grin tugged at his lip. "Do you need to make calculations?"

Ruby's eyes flew up to his, wide and startled, almost as if she had been expecting to see someone else sitting in his space. Her mouth tightened, and he regretted the gentle poke.

"No," she said. "Of course not." With a snap, she flipped the cover of the sketch book closed and set her pencil down atop it.

"My apologies," he began, but she interrupted him.

"Are not necessary." She drew her shoulders back, brushed imaginary lint away from her lap, and glanced around for Mrs. Baumgartner. "You should find out what you can about the town and its inhabitants. I will see what our hostess—or her girls—can tell us. Perhaps you might see if a general store or some similar establishment can offer any insight into the town's troubles?"

Curse it, Trip. If you had kept your fool mouth closed, you might have found out everything you need to know about the woman right then.

Then again, how much did he need to find out, exactly? They were here to do a job together, that was all. No one in St. Louis had said a word about assigning him a partner for good. All he had to do was figure out how to work with the woman this once, and then he'd be on his way.

He didn't know whether he hoped the case would wrap up soon or drag out for weeks. Ruby Silver was having some kind of effect on him, and she'd been in town less than a day.

Standing, he gathered his hat off the bench beside him

and gave his new, temporary partner a short bow.

"Shall I see you at dinner then, so as to compare notes?" she asked. Her tone was much more formal than when she had been considering taking measurements inside the bank, and he found that he preferred the other voice.

Even if he was more than a little certain that voice had not been meant for him.

He knew it was foolish to get involved with one's partners. Although it might not be forbidden by the company, it wasn't exactly encouraged, either. Theirs was a dangerous business, and a nomadic one. He never knew from week to week where he would be, or what he would face.

And that's a fine excuse for avoiding involvement with someone outside the business.

What about avoiding the woman with whom he had been partnered?

Watching her speak quietly to the girl wiping down the trestle-tables, he suspected he already knew the answer to that: he would not have to avoid her. She would avoid him enough for the both of them.

CHAPTER FOUR

It had been a while since Ruby had actually forgotten herself enough to lose track, even for a brief time, of Flint's absence.

Those moments usually came in the morning as she was waking up. All too often, she still found herself reaching across the bed for him, or listening for the sound of him moving around the room.

Now, once again in her bedroom, she pressed her face into the counterpane spread across the bed and bit back tears.

The room was airless and hot. She wouldn't be able to stay in here long.

Only long enough to collect herself.

Then, perhaps, she could lose herself in the work.

And either way, she would see to Lakota when she was done. Then she would lie down and rest before supper in order to remain awake all night.

"With any luck, I can rid the townspeople of their ..." What had that word been? Something *geist*. A noisy ghost, Mr. Schmidt had told them. Her German skills were sorely lacking—but if German immigrants were picking up spiritual riders like that and bringing them to Ruby's part of the world, she apparently needed to brush up on the language.

Her mind firmly centered once again in the task before her, she stood straight and smoothed out the blanket.

"I can do this. I can do anything I set my mind to."

Smartest woman Flint had ever met.

A crooked smile, backed with pain, made its way across her face.

And while I'm at it, I think I'll go take those measurements Mr. Trip Austin dismissed so readily.

* * *

"Have you noticed any pattern to the ... poltergeist's ... appearances?" Ruby glanced down at the sketchpad, where she had been prepared to jot down anything of note as she spoke to the mayor's wife and the women who regularly joined her for tea.

The page remained blank.

Truth be told, Ruby would rather have been conversing with Mrs. Baumgartner's whores.

For that matter, they might have been more forthcoming with details.

Not that the townspeople of Rittersburg had attempted to hide anything, as far as Ruby could tell. The woman whose drawing room Ruby currently occupied—married to the bank president, Mr. Schmidt—was perfectly pleasant, if perfectly dull. Nothing about her seemed at all out of the ordinary.

The quiet preceding this morning's flying-glass incident had actually been a lull between two attacks by the spirit, Ruby had discovered. That she had arrived in time for that quiet period was the cause of much speculation among the townspeople, though Ruby herself was as likely to mark it down to malevolence as luck.

There was something not quite right about this ghost, however. It wasn't performing like any specter she had ever encountered before.

Not for the first time that day, she wished she had Flint's expertise to fall back on. Rather idly, she wondered exactly what Trip's expertise was. Rubbing one hand across her forehead, she closed her sketch pad.

Mr. Austin, she reprimanded herself. It would not do to get lazy, to fall into the habit of calling him by his given name—or worse, his nickname. It would, however, be useful to discover what, if anything, he had found out during his time in town.

"Thank you, Mrs. Schmidt," she said, standing more abruptly than she had intended to.

"Ja, yes, of course," the woman of the house said, scrambling to cover for her ill-mannered guest. "You will of course let us know if we may help you in any way?"

The other women bobbed and nodded, and Ruby took her leave.

As she moved down the front steps, a girl, perhaps nine or ten, stepped around the corner of the building and glared up at her.

"Hello," Ruby said, keeping her tone light.

The girl narrowed her eyes.

"Were you looking for me? Can I assist you in some way?"

"No one wants you here." The girl's voice echoed oddly, in a way that made Ruby's heart catch in her throat.

"Pardon me?"

"I said, no one wants you here. You are unwanted." The girl's nostrils flared, and Ruby backed away, glancing briefly from side to side to see if anyone else had seen the exchange.

The street was as empty as it had been that morning, right before the poltergeist attack.

The child picked up a length of rope from the ground and began skipping, her voice a sing-song chant. "Unwanted. Uninvited. Unrequested."

As Ruby's steps picked up pace, the child began laughing maniacally. A pressure began building up in the air behind Ruby, whipping her skirts around her ankles.

"Unloved!" the child called out as Ruby scurried around a corner, leaning against the building to catch her breath as the sudden wind died down.

When she peered around the side of the building again, the little girl was peacefully jumping rope.

Mrs. Schmidt's front door opened, and a maid called out something indistinguishable to the child, who answered in a normal voice.

No wind. No chant. No strange, echoing voices. Nothing.

There is nothing here like that.

It was a coincidence. It had to be.

There was nothing at all to connect Rittersburg to the church.

Nothing other than Ruby herself.

* * *

By the time she reached the boarding house, she had a full-blown headache. Her hands shook when she closed the door behind her and reached up to untie her bonnet. She needed to relax, lie down for an hour or so and begin preparing to open herself to the Great Beyond in some meaningful way, in order to end this haunting.

As she hung her bonnet on the peg rack by the door, she considered what she knew so far. There had been a number of incidents, and everyone she had spoken to had seen something—much of it like the flying glass that had greeted her arrival in town. There had been a number of flying objects—often dangerous items, caught up in a maelstrom of wind and ethereal forces. Townspeople had been hurt, though none had been killed as of yet.

But a young girl had been knocked unconscious by a butter-churn that had sailed through the air and connected with her temple. It would not have taken much more force to cause lethal damage.

And yet no one had any definitive information to give her about sudden, unnatural deaths in the community—nothing that might normally lead to a haunting.

Ruby stepped up onto the staircase, her brow furrowed in thought, as the front door opened to admit Trip Austin.

"Ah, Miss Silver. I was hoping to find you in." He pulled his own hat off his head and tapped it against one leg, his thumb playing along the rim. "I would like to compare notes with you, if you are not opposed."

"Not at all." Although she wouldn't have said as much, Ruby was glad to have someone with whom to spin theories. No matter how often she spoke to Flint now, his persistent quiet—even in the face of her almost nightly séances in the beginning—left her feeling as if she were speaking to herself all too often.

"Shall we retire to the drawing room?" she asked, "Or would you prefer the garden?"

He glanced around. "I think the garden. At least for now."

That last had a more ominous sound to it than Ruby would have liked, but she preceded him out of the main house and took the same seat she had occupied earlier.

"You learned something?" she finally asked, after he played with the brim of his hand for several silent moments.

He set the hat aside, rapped twice on the trestle table, and folded his hands in front of him. "Tell me about your partner—and the demon that supposedly killed him."

* * *

Ruby froze in place, only her gaze flicking along the path to an exit giving away the fact that she had heard Trip speak at all.

Even if he had not seen the calculation behind her stare, though, he would have known that she had made out his words perfectly clearly.

This was not the stillness of calm. It was the stillness of a hunted animal—possibly even a wounded one, trying desperately to find its way into the safety of a bolt-hole and finding no path to salvation.

"My partner?" Her voice remained soft and unshaken.

But Trip had seen that expression in her eyes.

"Flint Donahue."

Ruby didn't exactly close her eyes, but her blink lasted a heartbeat too long to be natural.

Trip glanced around to make sure no one was around to hear him speak. "And you're Rowan Argent."

"Not anymore." Her words came out strained and raw with pain.

"You were in that church up in New Mexico with him, weren't you?"

Now she closed her eyes in earnest and nodded, a single tear gathering at the corner of her eyelid before she dashed it away. When she opened her eyes again, she had clenched her teeth. "Does it matter to you what I call myself?"

He shrugged. "I don't care, but our employers might."

"The Tremayne Agency knows exactly who I am." She all but hissed, leaning in so her face was close to his. "I am Ruby Silver, medium and half-competent exorcist. I have no other ties to those who hunt the spirit world, and when this town is cleared of its haunting, you and I will go our separate ways."

"What about the demon?" Trip asked, ignoring her last claim. "Rumor had it you were dead. Is it possible your demon survived, too?"

The air around Ruby seemed to thicken with anger, but she didn't answer.

Well, Trip wasn't new to this investigation game.

Time to change tactics.

Chewing on one side of his lip, Trip kicked his legs over the bench and spun around so that he sat with his elbows leaning back on the table. Picking up his hat, he dropped it down onto his head and leaned back to stare up into the bright blue sky, with its puffy white clouds—very similar to the ones that had been in the sky that morning when he had seen Ruby—Rowan—whatever her name was—do her trick dissipating the storm of glass that had blown in on the town.

"Where did all that glass come from?" he asked.

"Pardon me?" Ruby blinked and shook her head.

"A glass storm suddenly blows up, a person's gotta figure, it's not exactly out of nowhere. This ain't exactly plate-glass window country, not even with that big, new, fancy bank going up in the middle of town. I got to wonder: where did all that broken glass come from?"

He glanced around the sky. "I'm also wondering where it went—and if the people there are wondering where it came from, too—but right now, I'm mostly thinking about where it might have come from. Because it's my experience that when the kinds of creatures we fight use things of this world to attack people, they take it from someplace nearby. Somewhere that's familiar to them. Safe, even."

When he glanced at her out of the corner of her eye, Ruby was nodding, so Trip kept talking. "While I was out doing my rounds today, I went to the church. It's got a lovely stained glass window. One. Perfectly intact. Not much else there unaccounted for—not glass, leastwise, not so's I could tell. That takes the church out of the reckoning, I think." A slight shudder shook her frame, and he paused, then spoke as gently as possible, given what he had to say. "And taking the church out of the equation pretty much removes that church-lovin' demon of yours, too, doesn't it?"

So prepared was he to hear her say *yes* that he was halfway through his next sentence before his brain caught up with him.

"No."

"Good. Then we will need…" He trailed off. "No? Your demon's not out of the reckoning?"

"I don't think so."

"Why not?"

"The bank manager's daughter was possessed when I left their house." He barely made out the words, her voice was so harsh and dry.

Trip ducked down until he was certain she was looking into his eyes. "Was it the same demon who killed your partner?"

She nodded, eyes wide. "I think maybe it was."

"And what did it say to you?"

"That I am not wanted here."

CHAPTER FIVE

"We need to track this manifestation to its source." Trip managed to sound calm, but his eyes on her were troubled.

Ruby bit her lips closed and played with a sliver of wood that she had worried free from the tabletop.

Exactly how much did he know about the incident in New Mexico? How much of the story had gotten out?

Hunters talked.

How much of what they had said was true? When Ruby—still Rowan, then, before she had undergone the whitewashing of her past that the Tremayne Agency had sworn would hold up to almost any scrutiny—when Rowan had come reeling out of what was left of that tiny silver-mining town up the mountains, she had been virtually incoherent.

It had taken her days to find her way to the lowlands, even longer to get to a safe-house.

At the time, she had simply been thankful the demon hadn't followed her.

Now... now she wasn't certain that it hadn't.

Can I even tell the difference any longer between a noisy ghost and a demon?

Have I lost my edge?

"Has he been playing some kind of game with me?" she whispered, pinning the splinter to the table and holding it down tight, as if by keeping it still she might halt the demon's actions. "Did it know where I was the whole time?"

Crossing his arms over his chest, Trip regarded her through narrowed eyes. "Maybe." He shrugged. "Hard to tell, really. In any case, if it's really here, it's almost certainly connected to the thing the townspeople are calling a *poltergeist.*"

Panic bubbled up in her throat, clawing away at her insides like an acidic compound. "If it's the demon, I can't beat it."

"Of course you can." Trip's brows drew down in a V over his eyes. "I saw what you can do out there in the street this morning, Ruby. You have real power."

"Not enough." Her voice scraped its way out of her chest. He didn't understand. She had known he wouldn't.

"Then I can help." When Trip stood up and moved around the table to sit next to her, it was all she could do to keep from flinching away. No one had come this close to her since she had left Flint stretched out, cold and still, on the altar in the church and set it ablaze behind her.

Now, this man's shoulder bumping against hers felt like an imposition, the weight of his expectations folding in on her, pinning her to the bench she sat perched upon. As if, were he to stand up and leave, she would shoot into the air and fly away with a pop, much like the flying glass she had sent into the sky earlier that morning.

Oh, to fly away and be nothing but glass.
Unbroken glass.
Unbreakable.

Or the stone she had named herself after. Even the tree her parents had chosen as a namesake.

One of the girls came out from the house into the garden just as Ruby whimpered. The girl jumped, startled. "Are you well, Miss?"

"I am fine. Thank you, Heidi."

Trip was right. Ruby had enough power to potentially help someone, and in the end, that mattered more than saving her own skin.

Flint would have agreed.

The sound of her heart pounding in her chest echoed dully in her own ears. Since the demon had spoken to her, everything about this job terrified her. And no matter what she tried to think about, the image of Flint's motionless body lying atop the altar kept superimposing itself over her mind's eye.

"You realize that our chances of surviving are low, correct?" she asked.

Trip nodded.

"And that the spirit we're tracking may not be a spirit at all, but a minor demon?"

He nodded again.

"Very well." Ruby inhaled sharply and brushed her hands together as if wiping away something unpleasant. *In a sense, I suppose I am.*

She took a moment to regain her balance.

If I die, I can rejoin Flint.

The thought steadied her.

Suddenly, even losing to the demon seemed an acceptable outcome, if it meant she could be with Flint again.

"Do you have any experience dealing with demons?" she asked the cowboy sitting next to her. For the first time since that morning, she closed her eyes and let her inner vision—the one she used to call up the powers she held within herself—take over. When she opened her eyelids again, the world around her seemed to glow with an inner light, living beings creating their own illumination in the falling dusk.

This time, she prepared herself to look at Trip with her Second Sight. Even so, she wasn't ready for the after-effect his image, burned onto her retina. Everything else around her—and always, always people—held a gentle glow tinted with the hint of a color: a peaceful blue or a soft green, or even a red of rage or black of despair.

Not Trip.

He blazed an intense white, so bright it almost blinded her, so vivid it made her ill—a brilliant, nauseous white that dazzled her so completely it left her with a Trip-shaped hole in her vision.

And where their auras touched, her own aura fractured, erupting in all directions in a starburst of purest white—but ending in a rupture of the brightest shades of pinks and purples that she had ever seen.

"Like the desert at sunset," Trip whispered, and Ruby realized she had taken his hands to steady herself, and he had done the same, so that they clutched each other's hands, their foreheads almost touching.

"You can see this?" she asked.

"The colors? Yes."

"They're our auras." Lifting one hand away from his, she slid it out to one side, then back in gently, watching trails of light flutter away behind it.

"Is this normal?"

"Not at all." Ruby brought her hand back in and began working at spooling the energy she felt swirling through their auras. "But I might be able to use it."

For the first time in months, Ruby's interest was piqued. If this combined-aura force could be harnessed, it might help them combat the demon.

Or even merely the poltergeist.

Odd how the town's strange haunting, so pressing that morning, had so quickly become secondary in the face of one of Hell's Knights.

"Should we try to understand what this is?" Squeezing his eyes closed, Trip shuddered. "Is it dangerous?"

"Oh, almost certainly." With her other hand, she worked at drawing out and dispensing the force she had built up.

"You don't sound particularly concerned."

"I am merely attempting to concentrate." If she focused her attention, she could pull the energy of this strange combined aura, as she did any power source.

"Stand over here," she directed Trip, standing and moving to the far side of the garden, drawing him with her.

"Why?" he asked, but he followed her, anyway.

"Because I need to determine if you are any good on your own, or if I will need to remain physically connected to you in order to make use of this new power."

* * *

Ruby was perhaps the strangest woman Trip had ever met. Mere moments before, he had been convinced that she was about to bolt—to take what she knew of the demon that had tracked her to this town and run, as fast as possible.

She had refused to acknowledge her name.

Rowan Argent.

Even after he had put it all together, Trip had wasted a good chunk of time telegraphing the St. Louis office to confirm that he was really working with *the* Rowan Argent.

She and her partner were legends among the hunters who still worked this part of the country—almost as renowned for their determination to remain freelance as for their demon-hunting abilities.

When they went missing in New Mexico, everyone assumed they both died in the fire that had wiped out an entire mountain town.

That she was here—and more, that the demon that had gotten her partner had possibly followed her—meant nothing good.

But it also meant that there was almost certainly a connection between the German town's poltergeist and the hell-beast Ruby had fled from.

Trip suspected it was going to be up to him to figure out what that connection was—and more to the point, how to use it to put the demon down for good.

Even if Ruby was terrified that she wouldn't be able to do it.

She'll simply have to.
We will do it together.
Somehow.

CHAPTER SIX

Trip closed his eyes and leaned his head back. "Can we dismiss this hellish light?" he asked.

"Mm-hmm," Ruby said absently, tilting her head and frowning at the pattern the light made when she spun it around her fingers. "Of course." With a single tug on one glowing strand and a spin of her forefinger, she seemed to snap the light away, much as she had the glass that morning.

The afterimage still burned against the back of Trip's eyelids, but at least the bright glare was gone. He rubbed the back of his hands against his eyeballs. "Were you able to determine anything of any significance?"

She had spent at least half an hour moving the two of them around the garden as the sun dropped toward the western horizon, testing her control over the light element first as they touched, then as they stood progressively farther apart.

"It certainly behaves more responsively when our auras are touching." She frowned, flicking against his shirtfront with one annoyed finger.

"You knew that within the first two minutes."

"Yes, well, it doesn't hurt to ascertain these things through trial and evidence," she responded primly, folding her hands over one another and peering at him like a displeased schoolmarm.

Trip's bark of laughter echoed through the courtyard. "Very well, ma'am. What else did you learn in the course of your experiments?"

With a rueful smile, Ruby dropped down into a chair and relaxed the proper miss act. "Not much. The power itself seems to be very similar to what I used this morning to direct the glass storm. This is more intense and has the potential to offer more strength, but that possibility seems to be in direct correlation to how much you and I interact as I try to use it."

"If we work together, we're stronger and better?" Trip's voice, always something of a drawl, slowed down even more now.

"In general, yes." Ruby chewed on her bottom lip as if trying to decide how much to say.

"Out with it." The circular motion of Trip's hand betrayed his impatience. "What is your concern?"

Shaking her head, she rubbed her own eyes. "I am not certain that this doesn't have the potential to wipe out anyone who uses it. I am, in a very real way, playing with fire here. I am almost certain that it is this kind of power that the demon has at his disposal. Using it ourselves has the potential to be exceptionally dangerous."

"What about the poltergeist?"

Tapping her fingers against the trestle-table, Ruby worked out how best to say something she found difficult to put into words. "I'm not at all certain that the poltergeist and the demon are actually different spirits."

"What makes you say that?"

She blew out her cheeks. "Every entity—whether a person or a spirit or a manifested guide from the Other Side—has a specific feeling. A way of behaving. One of my teachers called it a signature. Having once felt your aura, I will always recognize it as yours because it maintains this specific … texture."

"Does the demon not have one?"

"No, that's not it at all. The demon's aura is absolutely specific. In fact, it's virtually identical to the one I felt on the poltergeist this morning."

"Is it possible for two different … beings? … to have the same aura?"

Twisting her mouth up in a little moue of denial, Ruby

shook her head. "Not in my experience."

"So you're arguing that the poltergeist and the demon are the same creature?"

"I'm not sure, but they're too similar for my comfort."

So after all that experimenting, they were right back to where they had started?

Of course.

"We need to trace the manifestation back to its source," Trip announced again. Perhaps this time Ruby would agree.

"Mmm. Yes. I suppose so," Ruby replied. Clapping her hands once, she stood up and clasped them together in front of her. "Would you care to join me?" she asked brightly, the hint of a teasing smile playing around the corners of her mouth.

Trip sighed and shook his head, but he too was smiling. "Lead on, madam," he said with a bow and a flourish.

If I'm going to go down fighting a demon, I might as well do it with a smile on my face...

And a pretty woman at my side.

All in all, I've heard of worse fates.

* * *

Before they left, Ruby stopped by her room to gather a carpet bag of supplies, then led Trip to the middle of Main Street, in front of the bank. Had this been any other Texas town at this time of evening, now that the worst of the sun's punishing rays had dropped almost below the horizon, there would have been a few couples out strolling along the new-cut streets, nodding to one another and perhaps stopping to visit.

Rittersburg stood silent and still, as if the residents of the town were waiting for the inevitable attack.

She glanced at the light beige dirt at her feet, her boots kicking up a miniature dust-storm as she walked.

"There's no glass left at all," Trip observed.

"There wouldn't be. I sent it all together, through a

process rather like magnetism. Like attracts like. All the glass shards traveled together."

"All the glass shards in town, or simply all the ones in that storm?"

She chewed on her bottom lip, attempting to sort through a conflicting welter of images from the morning's work. "All pieces of glass connected to any in that storm."

"So any pieces that were not flying around, but came from the same larger broken glass?"

"Would have traveled with the shard-cloud, yes."

"Do you have any way of tracking their origin?"

"Possibly." Rolling her shoulders back, Ruby closed her eyes, centering her weight on her feet and allowing what she privately thought of as *the energy of the earth* to roll through her. As she inhaled and exhaled, that power took root deep in her soul, sparking heat in the touch-points her mentor in England had called her "chakras," after an old tradition from India.

When she had drawn on her power to banish the glass-storm, Ruby had, without thought, sent an almost electric energy, like lightning, shooting through those points of connection. This, however, was the first time she had consciously drawn on them in longer than she cared to remember.

It felt like blowing cobwebs away from a roomful of windows. Gently, Ruby brushed the dust of disuse away from the windows of her soul, preparing to allow more than a simple lighting-crack of radiance shine through. When she had finished mentally rubbing away the grime, she imagined pushing open shutters and allowing whatever was waiting to stream in.

As before in the garden, the glare of the light almost blinded her, and she made a tiny noise of resistance.

"What is it?" Trip asked, and Ruby realized that he was hovering next to her, one hand on her elbow.

"Would you please take one step backward?"

When he moved away, she found that she had better control over the amount of power streaming through her, and she frowned. "As with our auras, your proximity intensifies the effect of the power I channel."

"Is that good or bad?"

"I'm not certain. It might come in handy." Her furrowed brow smoothed out as she closed her eyes again, sinking back into the image of her internal landscape as a room surrounded by glass windows, sparkling clean and streaming with sunlight. With a few more breaths, she drew upon her sense of the morning's glass shards as part of a moving storm, traveling *from* two particular points, and drawn, she realized, specifically *to* her.

"That way, and that." She pointed before opening her eyes, hoping to avoid contaminating her sense of direction with any visual cues.

"The bank and ..." Trip paused, his own brow beetling with confusion for a moment. "The church?"

Ruby's sharp gasp drew his attention back to her, but she shook it off. "I'm fine. The church was where the demon chose to stage his final battle in New Mexico."

Why on earth had she thought she could use her gifts with impunity ever again? What had made her think the beast wouldn't track her down, find her again, send her after Flint?

"Ruby. Look at me." Trip's voice made its way through the haze of terror that had engulfed her momentarily. Her hands shook where he clasped them in his own.

"Can you examine the church with me?" He gazed into her eyes with his own, so dark and opaque, so different from Flint's. "If not, I can explore on my own."

With a steadying breath, she firmed her shoulders. "No. I need to do this. If the demon has truly followed me here, I need to help eliminate him. And if the threat is the poltergeist, or truly, anything other than the demon, my aid might still be invaluable. I am prepared to go with you."

"If you're certain."

She glanced at the tall steeple and the white clapboard building. Trip was right. This was not New Mexico. Even the building materials were different.

"I am absolutely certain." Nodding decisively, she squeezed his hands once before dropping them and striking out across the street toward the building. "Let's see if I can determine why the glass came from the church."

Trip nodded. "Yes. Let's go track down a poltergeist. Or maybe a demon."

* * *

Ruby was stronger than he'd thought. She seemed well-prepared to deal with the anxiety triggered by such a strong reminder of the events in New Mexico. She was one tough slip of a woman and he found himself admiring her more and more.

He had never gone up against a demon himself, but having heard tales of it from other hunters, he wasn't at all certain that he would fare as well.

Knowing that she was ready to face the monster that had defeated her before did not, however, erase the look of sheer terror he had seen in her eyes. He hadn't fully recognized it before, but it had been fear he had seen banked in her eyes before, from the first time she looked at him—a low-burning fire comprised of dread and grief that threatened to erupt at any moment.

She's Rowan Argent. Of course she's made up of misery and fright.

Not that anyone would know it to see her now, walking toward the church ahead of him.

The rays of the setting sun shot the sky full of pink-gold light, sparkling off the church's single stained glass window.

The broken glass hadn't come from the building itself.

Like the rest of the public buildings in the town, the church was undergoing renovations, its wooden exterior being faced with the chalky white stones of the region.

They stepped inside, the heavy door swinging shut behind them and blocking out the sunlight, and Ruby moved confidently up the center aisle of the nave to the chancel, where she stopped to light a candle.

"Come look at this," she said, motioning him forward.

Feeling as if he should somehow show more respect inside a church, Trip took off his hat and shuffled forward.

"No one else is here, Trip." Ruby's impatience hurried him forward, but she didn't offer any hints when he joined her.

"What? It's a tray, with a knocked-over cup."

"One perfectly empty, metal chalice. But look, there's a splash of wine over here, completely on the other side, facing the wrong direction to have come from this cup."

"So you think maybe there was a wine glass here?"

She nodded, closing her eyes and allowing her hand to hover over the spot for a moment. "Crystal, I think."

"One glass wouldn't have been enough to cause what we saw when we arrived."

"No." Ruby surveyed the domed ceiling above them, then began walking along the walls, holding her candle aloft and examining the darkened corners of the room in the dim, flickering light. "But the glass—all of it—came from inside here, I think. At least, it feels that way."

Trip took an unlit candle from the same stock that she had mined, and moved to light his candle from hers, planning to follow her lead and search for other sources of glass. As he tipped the wick toward the wavering yellow glow, however, the fire burst out in all directions, expanding in a sudden surge of heat.

Trip and Ruby sprang apart, and with a cry, Ruby flung the exploding candle to the floor. Burning globules of hot wax landed on Trip's arms where he had instinctively covered his face, leaving behind bright red circles where he shook them off.

At that moment, Trip realized that Ruby was no longer standing across from him. She had dropped to the floor, where she crouched, whimpering, her arms clasped protectively over her head.

Before he had time to stamp out the expanding circle of fire on the thin, red carpeting that covered the center aisle, the double doors at the entrance crashed open and a hot wind blew past him, whipping the tiny blaze higher.

Trip bent down to draw Ruby up and away from the flames, but eyes wide, Ruby stared past him at the fire, and Trip realized that she was repeating two words over and over.

"Not again."

CHAPTER SEVEN

Grabbing Ruby around the waist, Trip spun her away from the fire, setting her on her feet behind him before turning back to put out the fire on the carpet.

As the last of the flames died out under the force of his boots, an ominous rustling, creaking sound filled the church. Something thick and heavy flew past his head and crashed into the nearest wall. As it slid to the floor, he realized it was a hymnal.

The sound of the book hitting the wall jarred Ruby out of her terror, and she took hold of his hand. Over the sound of the hymnals rising into the air from the pews around him and flinging themselves through the air, she shouted, "Follow me."

Only one of the heavy books managed to deal him a glancing blow off one shoulder before Ruby had pulled him around the altar and through the door into the sacristy at the back of the building. He shoved the door closed behind them, leaning against it as several of the books slammed against it, the impacts thrumming through his body and underscoring their near-miss.

His eyes strained in the darkness.

"We need a match," Ruby said, and he heard her rummaging through something. The light flared and the sharp, sulfurous smell was quickly replaced by the scent of melting wax as she lit a candle and held it up while they examined their surroundings.

The storage room was small and lined with shelves.

No place for a demon or a poltergeist to hide.

He breathed easier for a moment, but a quick glance around the church's storeroom for religious items quickly brought his concern crashing back. There were far too many things in here for the town's ghost...poltergeist...demon... whatever was haunting them...to toss around. Trip didn't think it would take the creature long to get down to harassing the two agents where they were.

"Is there a back door out of this place?" he whispered.

"I don't think so," Ruby replied. Leaning toward the door, she narrowed her eyes. "I don't hear anything out there now. We could make a run for it."

Picturing the long aisle leading to the heavy doors, Trip shook his head. "Did the doors shut? I don't think we'll be able to open them to get out, even if we make it that far."

"How do you propose we get out, then?" Ruby asked.

Trip picked up a silver candlestick and hefted it in his hand. "There's a window on each side of the altar. We can break one and escape that way."

Ruby lifted the bag she had held on to—rather miraculously under the circumstances, Trip thought—and said, "But I haven't completed any banishing rituals yet. If this is not the demon, if it's merely the town's poltergeist, I might be able to exorcise it now."

"You don't think it's some sort of apparition, do you?"

She shook her head. "Not at all. I do, however, plan to be certain before terrifying these good people with tales of demons and hell-fire."

Despite a fast-growing desire to be gone from the haunted church, Trip did not actually disagree with Ruby. There was much to be gained from quickly expelling the ghostly force, and little to be lost.

Except, of course, possibly our lives.

"Very well," he muttered. "I will..." He paused, trying to determine how to complete that thought.

"Watch guard?" Ruby supplied.

"Yes." Testing the weight of the candlestick in his

palm again, he wondered exactly how he might use it against an unseen force that created tornadoes of broken glass and caused heavy hymnals to hurl themselves across otherwise empty churches.

"What kinds of supplies did you bring?" he asked. His own arsenal against the supernatural was relatively slim, concentrating as he usually did on finding ways to convince ghosts to leave this earthly realm rather than forcing them out.

"The usual." Ruby pulled out several stoppered glass jars. "Salt. Sage. Blessed candles, holy water, a Bible." She set the items out in front of her and began choosing from them, pulling out the stopper from one of the jars and gathering a handful of salt from it. Leaning around him as he stood with his back to the door, she sprinkled it across the threshold of the closed door, muttering what Trip assumed was a protective prayer. He wasn't certain—at her nearness, the strange rushing sound of his own heartbeat filled his ears, and he held his breath to stop himself from inhaling her scent.

This is no time to have your head turned by a woman, Austin.

And given what he knew about this woman and the partner she had lost, there was a good chance it would never be the right time.

Trip concentrated on watching what she was doing, instead, and breathed easier once she stepped back again. The sound of his pulse faded, and he focused his attention on listening for any sounds from outside the door.

In the main part of the church, he again heard creaking and rustling, but nothing heavy thumped against the door.

"There. That should hold us for a while. Now we need another match." She dove back into her carpet bag. When she held one up triumphantly, Trip didn't know whether to cheer or groan, so he settled for merely nodding.

As long as whatever she was about to do got them out of the church, Trip was willing to follow her lead.

* * *

- 53 -

Ruby pulled a half-burned smudge stick out of her bag. The bundle of sage, tied together tightly with hemp string at regular intervals, had belonged to Flint, and she had to bite the inside of her cheek to force herself to pay attention to the physical pain rather than concentrate on her memories of him using it at various sites they had worked together.

It wouldn't do to allow her grief to distract her while she completed the cleansing rituals. At best, she would make herself miserable. At worst, she might invite a negative spirit to attach itself to her or to the location, and she refused to leave the town worse off than it was when she arrived.

Instead, she concentrated on the Lord's Prayer as she first lit the smudge stick, then gently blew out the flame so that the herb continued to smolder, letting off a slow trickle of smoke.

There were potentially better prayers, but that one had the force of habit behind it, so she often defaulted to it. As she waved the sage in the air, she added her own requests for peace and cleansing, some aloud, but even more silently.

She pulled upon her own power to add force to the requests. At one point, she even reached out and touched Trip's arm to better access some of the additional power she was able to draw from him. He jumped a little at the contact, but did not attempt to pull away.

After she completed the exorcism ritual, she took a short break, then prepared to check her work. "If it was successful," she told Trip, "I won't be able to feel the manifestation's presence in the church."

Closing her eyes, she delicately placed one hand on Trip's sleeve. The connection between them flared bright behind her eyes, and with her sixth sense, she sent that additional energy questing out into the church.

"Anything?" Trip asked.

"Nothing yet," she murmured. The church itself felt shadowed and chill to her mystical senses, but that might be a remnant of the specter's presence rather than something imminently dangerous.

When that coldness became icy, though, Ruby gasped. Her sense of power flickered around the deep blackness of an ice-cold void in the church.

No. Not quite void.

In its depths pulsed a malevolent fire, a banked inferno waiting to blaze to life again.

"Is it still here?" Trip's voice drew her attention back to the sacristy.

"Yes," she whispered. "But it seems to be disabled, at least momentarily."

"What does that mean?"

She took a moment to consider. "I think we should move now."

At that moment, the presence in the church renewed its attack against the door.

Apparently that freeze didn't last long.

"Or perhaps not," she amended.

The poltergeist—or maybe the demon, as Ruby was more and more inclined to believe—attacked with force. The sound of wood splintering and glass shattering echoed through the church, all of it slamming against the door that protected them, but with her salt line and her smudge stick smoke, all reinforced by the power of prayer in this holy place, there was little the evil spirit outside could do to get to them.

"I suspect we will be here a spell," Trip said, crossing his legs and dropping to the ground, camp-style. "Might as well get comfortable."

Not entirely possible in a dress, but Ruby would do her best.

The candlelight flickered, sending shadows crawling up the wall, but they seemed less creepy than they might have, had an invisible force not been attacking the other side of the walls.

Shadows don't hold much terror when there's an actual monster at the door.

"I have a question," Trip said after a moment.

Ruby nodded her permission, expecting something about the rituals she had performed, or perhaps how long their sanctuary might hold out against the entity's assault.

Instead, the agent stretched out on one side, apparently totally at ease, his head propped up on his elbow and his long legs crossed at the ankle. For the first time, Ruby realized that, although he might be young—certainly no older than she was, and much younger than Flint had been—Trip Austin was an attractive man.

She blinked to dispel the thought and focused on his question.

"How is it, exactly, that a renowned demon hunter like yourself ended up working as an agent—no, not just an agent, but a *junior* agent—for the Tremayne PSI Agency?"

A frown flitted across her face. How to explain that empty place after Flint died, that utter void where everything that made her a person should have been?

Oddly enough, here in this small closet—a tiny space stuffed full of religious relics, lit by one guttering candle, and beset by something monstrous from the outside—Ruby found herself able to say the words out loud, even if she wasn't able to look Trip in the eye as she did it.

It was a space for a lot of firsts, apparently.

"Flint was married, you know. Not to me." A quick glance at Trip caught an expression of surprise on his face, though he looked away quickly to try to hide it. "To hear him tell it, she was some harpy from back East who headed home the first chance she got. I don't know for sure, of course. Didn't care, either. As long as she wasn't out here, it was fine by me."

Trip was chewing that over, for sure. Those Tremayne Agency rules, with their focus on propriety, could have him all wound about over this. He finally gestured around the sacristy. "But you're a religious woman."

Ruby shrugged. "I'm a practical woman. I do believe in the Almighty. I've seen too much to think all that highly of the rest of it. We have ways of reaching out to the Great Beyond. We have ways of keeping order on this side. They're all simply tools, in the end."

Trip's expression turned thoughtful. Yes. Definitely better to tell him all of it now. If they continued to work together, he would need to know.

"Flint was older than me, too, though he never would tell me his real age." A small smile played around her lips. "He trained me in the art of demon-hunting. And it is an art. Part ghost-trapping, part spell-casting, part prayer, with a few special weapons thrown in for good measure.

"We were good together. The best. Everyone knew for that kind of trouble, you needed Argent and Donahue. Even some of the Indian tribes called on us for help a few times. We learned about smudging from them." She gestured at the bundled herbs.

Trip wanted to ask questions, they were practically written across his face, but she needed to get this out—she knew, deep down inside her soul, that it was important for her to tell him all of it.

"Your boss offered us jobs, you know. A standing offer from the mysterious Nat Tremayne himself."

"Or herself," Trip murmured, and Ruby laughed, but only a little.

"Or herself," she acknowledged. "We declined, of course. Everything was perfect. We loved our life, loved being together, loved being out here, free to take the jobs we wanted to take and keep working on clearing the entire land of whatever these creatures may be."

"You call them demons. Do you not believe that's what they are?"

She shrugged. "Close enough. They're from the other side, they have power, and they're evil."

"You have power, too."

"I like to think I'm not evil."

"So what happened?"

"We took the job in New Mexico." Ruby couldn't help but notice he hadn't engaged her claim that she wasn't evil.

Too much of that Agency training.

She thought of a line from one of the training manuals she had left behind, back in the room the Tremayne Agency had rented for her during her training stint in St. Louis: "Reputation is everything."

Looked like maybe Trip believed that.

That's why it's best to tell him all of it now.

Her voice lowered. "We were over-confident. So sure of being the best that we dropped our guards."

Outside the tiny room where they sat, a supernatural wind howled. In here, though, the still air seemed to pile Ruby's own words around her, an invisible mound packing her in like the wadding in a muzzle-loader, waiting for a spark to set off the gunpowder of her guilt.

The best she could hope for was to be aimed the right direction when it all exploded.

To keep from wounding Trip in the blast, she needed to be certain he understood.

"What happened in the church?" he finally asked when she remained silent too long, trying to find the words that would force him to see her for the danger she was, the risk she presented to him.

She had never told this story before, though, and in the end, the most she was able to do was give the barest recitation of events.

When she spoke this time, her voice was little more than a hoarse whisper. "We didn't prepare enough." God knew she had spent enough time since then going over all the things they hadn't done.

The litany pounded through her head: *no blessed circle, no pentagram, no invocation of the elements, no prayers.* The list went on and on.

She drowned out the internal noise by continuing her narrative. "Nothing we did worked. Not smudging, not salt, not silver. Flint's six-shooter *melted* in his hand." His remembered scream sent a shiver up her spine. "A fire broke out between us and the door, and the demon's face appeared in the flames." The more she spoke, the faster the words came, pouring out of her in a molten torrent of pain. "The heat drove us toward the altar. Flint grabbed my hand and shoved all his own power into me. He started saying something, either an incantation or a prayer, and whatever it was, it picked me up and threw me toward the door, over the fire."

She paused to take a breath, slowing again as she tried to decide what to say. "I tried to get back to him, but the flames blocked my way. Then I saw them. The demon had Flint stretched out on the altar, like some kind of sacrifice, and stood over him, a red-hot knife raised up, ready to plunge into Flint's heart.

"And the last thing Flint did, the very final action he took in this life, was to turn his head and look me straight in the eyes as he flung out his arm and used every last bit of his supernatural ability to throw open the church doors and hurl me out into the New Mexico night."

The supernatural wind outside the door had abated a bit, as if the fiend were listening to Ruby's story, too.

Maybe it was.

Let it, then.

Let the damned thing hear everything that powered Ruby's rage, her sorrow, her anguish.

Let it know that this time, I will not stop until I know for certain that it has been utterly destroyed.

She closed her eyes, tears pouring down her face, but her voice remained steady. "I passed out—maybe from the force of that much power hitting me at once, or maybe I hit my head when I landed. Either way, it was dawn when I woke up. The church was still standing. Inside wasn't as burned as I expected. Only a blackened circle around the altar—almost like the demon had gathered all that heat into himself and used it to keep Flint contained.

"In the center of that circle, nothing had burned." Her jaw clenched as she worked to get the next words out. "Flint lay stretched out, eyes shut, like he was sleeping. But so cold." She opened and closed her hand in memory.

Her next words were as cold as Flint had been. "I lit a match, dropped it, waited until I was sure it caught, and I walked away."

Opening her eyes, she captured Trip's gaze with hers. "I knew that demon was still out there—knew it in my bones—and I walked away. I rode hard and fast to the nearest train station, sold my horse, bought the first ticket out to St. Louis for me and Flint's horse, changed my name, and took a job with the Tremayne PSI Agency."

She took a deep breath. "That's why I'm going to do everything I can to kill that monster now. I won't let anything stand in my way, not even you. If you want to back out now, I won't blame you. This is a fight to the death."

Pausing, she made sure he was staring directly into her eyes before she spoke again, emphasizing each word as she did. "A fight I do not expect to survive."

CHAPTER EIGHT

Ruby clearly wanted Trip to condemn her for her actions, confirm the guilt she felt. He refused. He'd been a ghost hunter for the Tremayne Agency for a couple of years now, and he had never run across anything as terrifying as the scene she described.

Honestly, the presence thumping outside the door against his back right now was the most frightening one he had come across. Usually, he helped those dealing with a haunting determine what the spirit wanted—almost always some kind of understanding about how the specter had died—and urged the ghost to move on. If that didn't work, if the ghost was more determined, or more evil, than your average soul, he read a standard exorcism prayer and banished the shade from that place.

Until now, that had always been good enough. Oh, the Agency wanted him to do some kind of complicated hoopla, rituals and spells and such, but he had figured out pretty quick that it was mostly unnecessary, at least for your standard ghost-hunter without any special magical talent.

Someone like Ruby, on the other hand—that was a different story. He suspected she could take those Agency spells and twist them around into something downright powerful.

If it took anything more powerful than an exorcism, some salt, or a silver bullet, Trip wasn't your man.

Never before had he run into the kind of trouble he was beginning to suspect had followed—or possibly led—Ruby Silver, aka Rowan Argent, to this small town. He didn't know if he would be able to help her find her way out of that trouble, but he sure as the dickens—as sure as the very devil outside his door right now—was going to try.

And he wasn't about to let her die in the process, either.

Part of him wanted to tell her that, to meet her intensity with his own, but he wasn't a hero, and this wasn't some Beadle's Dime Novel, either. What was happening in this town was real, and it was deadly. There was no way to guarantee that either of them would survive the night.

For that matter, he had only known her one day. No matter how drawn he was to her, or how much he wanted to clear away the desolation in her eyes, he didn't have any evidence that he would be able to do that for her. Or that anyone would.

Instead of matching her penetrating stare, he stared at the floor for a moment, settled his hat back on his head, and said, in his best, drawn-out Texas drawl, "Well. If you're so almighty determined to see it to the end, I reckon I'll just have to join you."

Trip didn't look up, but her surprise reverberated through the tiny space.

"Are you sure about that?" she asked. "There's nothing holding you here."

"I took the job. I might not have known exactly what I was signing up for, but this isn't the first haunting I've investigated. I'm not some greenhorn. In fact, technically, I'm the senior agent, you're the junior agent. I'm supposed to say whether or not we stay to fight. And...." He paused, finally looking up to meet her gaze before continuing. "I've a mind to make sure this demon of yours never bothers anybody again." A hard knock against the door punctuated his statement.

Ruby closed her eyes and pressed her lips tightly together, then, as if coming to an important decision, nodded once, firmly, and said, "So be it. Understand, though, if we make it out of this town alive, we go our separate ways. I'm not looking to team up with another partner." Her voice dropped. "I won't."

"Understood."

She stuck out her hand as if to shake on a deal. As much as he hated to do anything that might seal this compact and bind him to an agreement that required him to part ways with Ruby, he also sensed that she wouldn't hesitate to abandon him if she thought he might renege on that arrangement.

When he took her hand, a shock shot through him, straight from his hand to his toes. Trip jerked back his hand, but it was too late—the covenant he had made with Ruby felt cemented into his very core. "So what would happen if I tried to follow you out of town now?" he asked.

The other agent didn't try to pretend she didn't know what he meant. "That pain you felt a moment ago? It would be nothing compared to what you would experience if you broke our agreement."

"Well," Trip muttered. "I guess no man's ever going to lie to you."

She shot him an exasperated look, but didn't bother to respond. Instead, she began packing her magical items back into her carpet bag, and Trip realized that the church had been quiet for several moments.

"I believe we can make a run for it now," Ruby said calmly.

Trip stood, picking up the last candle and moving it to a shelf where it seemed unlikely to catch anything else on fire. If he were more conscientious, perhaps he would blow out the flame before he and Ruby left the room. As it was, however, he planned to focus all his attention on getting the two of them out alive.

The church building be damned.

Or something like that.

"Ready?" Trip held his hand out to Ruby, who looped her carpet bag over her wrist, threaded her fingers through his, took a firm grip, and nodded. With his other hand, he signaled the count: *one ... two.* ... On three, he flung the sacristy door open and sprinted for the main church entrance, pulling her with him as he ran. The carpet bag dragged at their clasped hands, but neither let loose of the other.

They made it halfway down the aisle before a howling wind screamed through the building, sending objects flying. Trip ducked his head down, covering it with his free arm, but kept moving toward the heavy wooden doors. He risked looking up long enough to glance back at Ruby. She, too, had lowered her head toward the floor, but rather than protecting herself with her arm, she was waving it in a circle above her head, fingers flying in some complicated pattern—one that seemed to be offering them some protection from the various items sailing toward them, he realized, as a Bible bounced off some invisible barrier directly in front of his forehead.

"Thanks," he shouted over his shoulder.

"Keep moving," she replied.

Trip leaned into the increasing wind. "That's not as easy as it might seem."

"Neither is this." A cracking noise followed a particularly elaborate hand gesture, and Ruby shook her head. "If we can get to the open air, I think I can shut down the wind. Somehow, the building itself is powering all this."

Nodding, Trip redoubled his efforts, virtually dragging Ruby through the wind. Without her mystical interference, he was certain they would have been flattened against the back wall by now. But he heard her smooth alto voice repeating several phrases in what sounded like it might be Latin, and her incantation seemed to push against the unnatural wind that whipped around them, the words themselves expanding into a bubble around the two of them.

When they reached the doors, Trip pulled Ruby up beside him, and they each grabbed a door handle. Ruby shouted, "Hang on!" and made a chopping motion as she bit off the last of the incantation. The protective bubble around them dropped away, and the wind that had been pushing at them took over, shoving them backward, but helping them open the heavy church doors in the process.

As soon as they made their way outside, Ruby took up the chant once more. This time, Trip wrapped his arm around her waist to pull her outside.

Even in the midst of the chaos surrounding them, he noticed how perfectly she fit in his arms.

He shoved the thought away. There would be time for that later—if they survived this attack and rid the town of whatever was haunting it.

And if he was able convince her to let go of the dead man she still carried in her heart.

That might end up being harder than exorcising Rittersburg's "poltergeist."

With a final push, he propelled the two of them down the church steps and out into the dark, dusty street. Night had fallen completely while they were inside the building. Only a few lights flickered from inside the buildings. Despite the sound of the wind shrieking from inside the church—or maybe because of it—no one had ventured out to check on the two agents.

Apparently, though, Ruby's prediction had been right: once out in the open air, she was able to contain the supernatural wind inside the building. A slight glow seemed to cover the open doorway, a sheen like light reflecting from glass. And like glass, it provided a protective shield.

As he watched, the wind inside the church began to die down, leaving behind only a jumble of ripped books, broken candles, and various tumbled items atop the burned flooring.

When the wind had completely abated, Ruby said, "I can't tell what is the demon's doing, and what is being caused by the poltergeist. For all I know, they're the same thing."

"So how can we find out?"

"We need to talk to some more people, find out everything we can about these poltergeists."

Trip's mouth twisted to one side. "I wasn't getting much of any use from anyone earlier. I'm not sure who to talk to about it, if they all go mule-stubborn when we try to get the story out of them." He dug the toe of one boot into the hardened dirt below his feet, working a small rock out of the ground and kicking it, sending it skittering toward the now-quiet church.

Ruby steepled her hands together and tapped them against her mouth as she chewed on her bottom lip for a moment. "I think," she finally said slowly, "that it might be worth it to skip trying to talk to the elders of the town."

"You thinking the kids might have something of use to tell us?"

"When I was leaving Mr. Schmidt's home earlier, a young girl spoke to me in the voice of the demon. I think that the young are more malleable, and therefore more easily drawn to the Other Side. We might be more likely to get real answers if we talk to them first."

Trip nodded. "Any of Mrs. Baumgartner's girls young enough, you think?"

"Perhaps. We can certainly begin there."

Despite their apparent agreement, though, neither of them moved toward the boarding house.

"Does something about all this strike you as odd?" Trip's cadence slowed even further than usual as he gestured, taking in the entire town. "For a place all beset by these noisy ghosts, it sure does seem awful quiet all the time."

"Except, of course, for when their poltergeists are attacking *us*."

"Exactly."

Ruby gazed thoughtfully around the main street. "The interior of the bank had a number of chips in the marble from earlier attacks."

"But not the church." The same church that now appeared utterly quiet again.

"No," Ruby agreed. "The church seemed untouched until our arrival. The glass attack appeared to originate with my appearance in town."

"That seem a mite peculiar to you? 'Cause it does to me. Nothing like any ghost I ever encountered before."

"I have been assuming that this haunting's oddities were a result of either its German origins or its demonic nature. But you're suggesting that there is perhaps another reason?"

"Or at least more to it than that."

"Another dimension, would you say?"

Nodding, Trip pressed his lips together to make a slight popping noise before he replied. "I might say exactly that, in fact."

A slow smile spread across Ruby's face as she regarded him—the first he had seen on her. Not enough to kill that desolation deep in her eyes, but perhaps the barest beginnings of a thaw in a frozen wasteland.

Or rain in the desert.

Trip had seen the desert after rain, all its glorious profusion of blooming and multiplying.

Somehow, he felt certain that there was equal life waiting in the depths of Ruby Silver's soul—if only he could find a way to open the right floodgates.

He realized that he had been holding her gaze for too long, but she didn't seem any more inclined to break this tenuous connection than he was, at the moment.

"Mr. Austin," she finally said, her beautiful alto voice smooth and soft, "I do believe that I might enjoy working with you, after all."

With that, she turned and headed toward the boarding house.

Then again, maybe I'm the desert and she's the rain.

He hastened to follow her.

* * *

As Ruby walked along the path that led from the main road to the boarding house, she found herself thinking aloud. "Mr. Schmidt put in the request to have a Tremayne PSI Agent sent out. And yet, when I spoke to his wife, she told me nothing of any use."

"Some men don't confide in their wives," Trip offered.

"True, and yet. ..." Ruby trailed off, her brow creasing as she tried to tease out all the implications. "Outside their home is where I was approached by the child who was, I am fairly certain, demon-possessed."

"But the little girl didn't do anything other than talk to you?"

"Nothing. In fact, the possession seemed to end almost as quickly as it began. As if. ..."

"As if?" Trip prompted.

"Almost as if the demon possessing her was unable to maintain his control."

"If it's the same demon that you and Flint fought in New Mexico, then how did it get here?"

Ruby shrugged. "How do demons travel anywhere?"

"You saying you don't know?" He arched one brow at her, and she found herself oddly charmed by his teasing.

"That is precisely what I am saying. Sometimes, they seem to travel by means of possession—by taking the body of a person and riding it, much as one might ride a horse. Other times, they must travel in spirit form, or by some means we do not currently understand."

Trip scuffed his boots along the ground as they walked, kicking small stones out of the way as he thought. "So what's the connection between Rittersburg's poltergeists and this demon of yours?"

"I am beginning to fully believe that they are one and the same." She managed to keep her voice steady, but at the thought of facing the fiend that had murdered Flint, her heart began to pound and a chill sweat broke out along the back of her neck.

"If that's the case—and I'm not saying it isn't, but if that is the case, then why go through the trouble of hiding it?" The more interested he became in the case, the more Trip's deep Texas drawl came out, as if he were forgetting to moderate the way he spoke.

Could that be true? Was Trip Austin attempting to sound less Western than he actually was?

Why would a Texan in Texas attempt to hide his native accent?

A mystery for another time. The man is not your focus, she admonished herself. And yet her interest in him had grown over the last hours.

The thought made her stomach clench, as if by merely noticing another man she might be showing disloyalty to Flint.

Don't be stupid, Ruby. Flint would want you to ...

To what?

To find someone else? To go on?

To live.

Her breath hitched in her chest as the words echoed in her mind, almost as if in Flint's voice.

"You alright?" Trip was too perceptive for his own good. Or at least for hers.

"I'm fine." She lengthened her stride as they came in sight of the boarding house. "I believe we should continue our discussion inside."

As they approached the front door, though, she slowed. "Have you noticed anything about the serving girls here?"

"They're all young and pretty?"

Ruby waved that away. "Yes, yes. I'm well aware that they are prostitutes, despite Mr. Schmidt's reassurances. It's not that." The upper windows were mostly dark, though candles flickered in a few. "It's the fact that they are all so *cheerful.*"

Trip's features were obscured by the gathering darkness, but Ruby felt his gaze settling on her as he tried to follow her thought processes. "They seem well treated enough."

"When you received your assignment to join me here, what information were you given? What were the exact words of the message you received sending you here?"

"I was up in Fort Worth. I got a telegram that said. ..." Now he was the one who trailed off for a moment. "It said that I was to join a new junior agent in Rittersburg. The next line was 'Town overrun by ghosts.'"

"Did that seem unusually precise language for our employer to use in a telegram?"

Trip laughed, a sharp bark of sound in the soft night air. "It seemed awful particular for a Tremayne telegram. Downright detailed, in fact."

"That was the wording of my communiqué, as well." She gestured expansively. "Despite our experiences upon our arrival and in the church tonight, does this, in fact, seem like a town that has been 'overrun' by the unhappy spirits of the dead?"

Trip frowned, and even in the dark, she saw him shake his head as he stared at the boarding house.

"In fact," Ruby continued, "I would go so far as to say that, although the townspeople of Rittersburg appear to be avoid us, they don't seem to be particularly haunted, at all."

"They don't even seem particularly scared," Trip agreed.

"There is more to this than we know." Ruby's foot tapped impatiently against the ground. She didn't like mysteries—not the earthly kind, anyway. She preferred her unknowns to be connected to the Great Unknown, the Other Side, that part of the world that was largely unseen.

She had to admit, however, that discussing the evidence of the town's lack of haunting with Trip had distracted her enough to calm the over-fast beating of her heart. The coppery taste of fear had faded from her mouth.

For a minute, it had almost felt ... not familiar, exactly. Flint would have pushed Ruby to come to her own conclusions, then come up with a definite plan of action.

But discussing the case with Trip was comfortable.

Perhaps even comforting.

Acknowledging that didn't get her any closer to understanding the issue at hand, however.

"I believe," she said, "that I might have a plan to discover what the good ladies of the Baumgartner Gasthof und Biergarten can tell us. How good are you at acting?"

"Acting?" Trip asked, startled.

"Yes. I am going to need you to follow my lead."

"Well, I can sure give it a shot." Amusement laced his words.

Ruby grinned, true delight shooting through her for the first time in months. "Excellent. Gather the girls and Mrs. Baumgartner, and meet me out back, in the biergarten."

CHAPTER NINE

"I need to hold a séance," Ruby announced, her blond hair flying around her face in the breeze in a way that made Trip's hand itch to smooth it back. "It's the only way we're going to trace all of these spirits back to their sources."

"You're absolutely certain there's more than one ghost?" He managed to keep his hands at his sides by looping his thumbs through his gun belt.

The girls of the house stood around them in a loose semi-circle, eyes wide, mouths agape at the two agents. Mrs. Baumgartner stood some distance behind them, arms crossed over her ample bosom as she scowled.

That one's a skeptic.

If anyone could make a believer out of her, it was Ruby Silver, aka Rowan Argent.

"No, I'm not at all certain of the number of spiritual presences in Rittersburg," Ruby was saying. "That is why I absolutely must hold a séance. I fear these German poltergeists act more demonic than ghostly, and I am finding it difficult to exorcise them." She paused, chewing on one corner of her bottom lip. Trip's hands tightened on his belt involuntarily as he stared at her mouth, mesmerized by the way her tongue swept the spot her white, even teeth had been.

She was pausing for effect, Trip was sure of it, and yet he found himself mesmerized by her.

This does not bode well for maintaining my sanity.

"A demon's influence is absolutely at play in this town," Ruby continued, shaking her head. "But I can sense some other presence, too. Possibly more than one. If Mr. Austin and I are going to save Rittersburg, we will need to deal with both the demonic and the phantasmic manifestations." She nodded firmly, making eye contact with each of the women standing around her. "And we will need your help to do so."

That was the first time she had used the term *we* to describe working against the shadowy forces they faced. Trip wasn't certain she actually realized it—either that she had avoided grouping herself with him before, or that she had done so now—but he had become acutely aware of the way she avoided the word whenever possible. Her use of it now lightened something in his heart that he hadn't even known had grown heavy. Even if this was mostly play-acting, he didn't think she was entirely faking it, either.

"What can we do to help?" one plump, round-eyed young woman asked.

Ruby dropped into the role of dreamy mystic without hesitation, her eyes focusing on something far away and her voice taking on a distracted cadence. "Ah, yes. Remind me of your name, my dear?"

"Laura," the eager volunteer offered.

"Yes, of course. Laura. Thank you so much. I will need a table, preferably round, though any will do, covered with a table cloth and surrounded by the number of chairs necessary to seat as many of us as will comfortably fit. This should all be in a darkened room. No more than two candles, please. In the center of the table, please place a salt cellar and a glass of pure well-water."

Trip blinked at the oddly specific list. Ruby had both salt and water in her carpet bag of tricks. He had seen them when they were closeted together in the church.

If he hadn't been watching her so closely, he might have missed the way her eyes flickered toward him.

Apparently this was part of whatever game she was playing.

He hoped his playacting ability was up to following her

lead.

The majority of the girls scattered to do Ruby's bidding. Trip and Ruby were the only guests in the Gasthof; Trip suspected the women were eager for a bit of excitement, and a séance certainly offered to provide that.

A few of them hung back, however. One of those lingered approached Ruby. Though her tone was polite enough when she spoke, it was also determined. "I'm very sorry, Miss Silver, but I am not willing to risk my immortal soul by participating in one of these devil-rituals."

Mrs. Baumgartner snorted. It seemed the madam of the house was as skeptical of religion as she was of other supernatural possibilities.

Ruby remained calm and polite. "Of course, dear. I would ask that you, along with anyone else who prefers to forgo participating, stay together in a room as far removed from the séance as possible."

The religious objector, mouth open to speak again, paused to digest this request instead. Her mouth opened and closed several times.

She looks like a fish.

"Why?" she finally managed to get out.

"I want no spiritual interference." Ruby's tone, vague and almost wistful only minutes before, turned severe. "And should there be any dangerous manifestations, your best protection will be your absence."

"I see." The girl scuttled into the house, followed by her associates. Trip had to wonder what kind of mental agility was required for a person to be both a prostitute and a believer in scripture.

When Laura called them into the front parlor less than fifteen minutes later, he was surprised to see Mrs. Baumgartner follow them inside, and even more surprised when she took the chair next to Ruby's.

Trip sat directly across from his temporary partner at the far end of the oval-shaped table, one of the Gasthof's girls on either side of him.

The dim, flickering light of the two candles made it difficult to see expressions, but most of the women at the table were quiet.

Ruby stood in front of her chair. "When we begin in a moment, I will ask you all to join hands. Please, whatever might happen, do not break the connection. Our handclasp is the connection that powers our link to the Other Side. We must maintain that connection until I tell you otherwise."

Everyone around the table nodded. Ruby took her seat, checked that all the items she had requested were in place, and solemnly held out her hands to the women beside her. There was a brief rustling noise as everyone else clasped the hands of their neighbors.

Trip didn't know what Ruby had planned.

But whatever it was, it was bound to be spectacular.

* * *

Ruby stared at the water glass for a long, silent moment. Then she closed her eyes and slowed her breathing, waiting for the sense of peace that always flowed through her body during a séance. It took longer than usual, but it showed up, eventually, and she began the ritual prayer she always began with. She knew the specific words didn't matter, only her intention, but she also knew that using the same words over and over helped her manifest the power and protection she needed to do the work she had been hired to do.

Holding Mrs. Baumgartner's hand on one side, and Heidi's on the other, she let her voice echo from the hollow space inside her chest that tugged at her center, pulling her toward the world of the spirit, even as it also held her anchored here, in the world of the living.

"We pray for peace here now, in this circle. We pray for love here now, in this circle. We pray to be surrounded by light and love and peace. We pray for the blue light of defense to surround us. We pray for guidance from those who have passed on to the other side. We pray for the protection of those spirits who would shield us. We pray for our guardians of light to safeguard us from all harm. We pray for shelter and care as we seek to speak to those on the other side. Watch over us and guide us. In our Lord's name, we pray. Amen."

It was an unconventional prayer, to be certain, but the other members of the séance circle were conditioned enough by church attendance to echo her final word, so that the majority of the circle added their *Amen*s, adding strength and power to the request.

A cool breeze blew past her cheek, and to her left, someone gasped. Ruby drew in a calm breath, prepared to speak to whatever phantom had manifested itself in this house. Before she opened her eyes, though, she surveyed the room through her sixth sense, feeling out the intentions of the specter awaiting her attention.

Nothing evil.

Only good intentions.

Nothing negative awaited her. With an additional, deep breath, she opened her eyes and turned to face the spirit, prepared to begin communication.

Flint stood to one side of her, looking like he had every day of his life, wearing his usual battered brown hat—the same one Ruby had worn into town—and that gentle smile that was always only for her.

Ruby froze, her breath stalling in her chest, as if she had been dropped to the ground from a great height.

"Rowan," he said, his voice pitched low.

She gasped, dragging air into her squeaking, protesting lungs.

"Where have you been?" she demanded, and burst into tears.

* * *

Trip stared at the filmy outline of the man floating next to Ruby.

So that was Flint.

Older than I expected.

Her former partner had been enormous, a mountain of a man with steel-gray hair and broad shoulders. Assuming his shade was the same height he had been, Ruby wouldn't have even come to his shoulder.

And that was who showed up when she called upon the protective spirits that surrounded her.

I need to watch my p's and q's.

Trip didn't know how much those in the spirit world might know of what passed through a person's mind, but the stern look he was getting from Flint's ghost at the moment suggested that the other man's specter was well aware of Trip's designs on Ruby.

Trip held the apparition's gaze for a long moment, then tilted his head and tapped his forehead as if saluting against the brim of his hat. Flint nodded in return, then faced Ruby, and apparently began speaking, though Trip couldn't hear what he said.

It seemed as if Ruby heard, though. Her shoulders heaved a few more times with sobs, but then she nodded and blinked away the tears from her eyes.

"I will," she said, her voice echoing oddly in the room, as if she were the ghost, rather than Flint. The rest of the séance participants gripped each other's hands tightly, unwilling to let go of their human connections in the presence of the ghostly figure.

"And will you help?" Ruby asked. She didn't merely sound haunting, Trip decided, but haunted.

She *was* haunted, of course, and this was the ghost who preoccupied her, both with his presence and with his absence.

Flint's shade nodded, and turned to regard Trip again. This time when it spoke, Trip heard it, though he suspected no one else did.

"You will care for her," it announced, its eyes glowing with a strange blue light that added intensity to its words. "Protect her."

Once again, Trip nodded without speaking, but it appeared to be enough for the ghost, who spoke one last time to Ruby, then began to fade.

Ruby sobbed once, leaning toward Flint and looking for a moment as if she were going to break the circle's hand-held connection, but she subsided into her chair before taking a shuddering breath and closing her eyes again.

Trip glanced around the table. The participants, for the most part, looked terrified, but continued to cling to one another's hands.

Good enough, he decided.

Tears still glinting on her cheeks, Ruby began a low chant. "We call upon the spirits who guide us to protect us. We call upon those who surround us to show themselves. We call upon those on the Other Side to speak. We call upon those from the Great Beyond to commune with us. We call upon the spirits who guide us to protect us. We call upon those who surround us to show themselves. We call upon those on the Other Side to speak. We call upon those from the Great Beyond to commune with us."

The repetition of the lines became almost a background hum. Trip glanced around the room. Most of the women had closed their eyes and were beginning to relax into the droning sound of Ruby's voice.

He had been around enough ghosts, however, and had attended enough séances to recognize the building of power around them.

Ruby's chant was functioning like a spell, drawing upon the connected energies of the people holding hands around the table, building it up to a force that could open a gateway between this world and the world beyond.

Everything was going precisely as planned. Perhaps even better, as the appearance of Flint's ghost indicated that a connection had already been made.

Why, then, was Trip suddenly filled with a sense of dread?

He wasn't able to bring himself to close his eyes.

Hell, I'm barely willing to blink.

The tone of Ruby's chant changed abruptly, dropping to a low growl just as the temperature in the room plummeted.

No one else around the table seemed to notice.

This isn't good. Trip tried to extricate himself from the circle, but the girls on either side of him held his hand too tightly for him to get away.

Too tightly to be natural, for that matter.

He couldn't make out what Ruby was saying now, but he was certain the voice coming from her throat was no longer hers.

When he tried to stand, an invisible force pressed him back down into his chair, a ghostly wind howling just beyond his ability to hear it, but causing his ears to ache nonetheless.

At that moment, Ruby's head dropped backwards, and a booming laugh echoed from her throat. Around the table, every woman's eyelids popped open, and they all turned to face him in uncanny synchrony, their eyes rolled back in their heads, their gazes pale and blank.

"Foolish man." They all spoke at the same time, their voices blending into a chorus that would have sounded lovely, were it not for the eerie echoing sound that he knew came from the monster he knew controlled them. "You think to eradicate us. We are legion, part of this earth for all of time, but a fraction of the land you hope to conquer. We cannot be removed."

Ice-cold fear ran through his limbs. Whatever this thing was, they had underestimated it.

Or rather, he had. The desolation underlying Ruby's every action made even more sense now. It was more than grief, more than terror.

It was the knowledge that she would face something unconquerable and lose.

This was why she had told him she did not expect to survive the night.

Trip wasn't sure he did, either—not any longer.

No matter what, though, I still intend to do my damnedest to get us both out of here alive.

Even if "damned" turned out to be the perfect word.

The demon can pile on the agony. I will still fight to save my partner.

To save this woman he had begun to admire beyond any other he had ever met.

"Ruby," he said, then repeated her name louder. The demon's laughter echoed from every person around him as he began shouting for Ruby to look at him.

When she didn't respond, he slumped back in his chair in momentary defeat.

No. I will not give up.

"Flint," he said in sudden inspiration, sitting as straight up as the forces holding him down would allow. "Flint," he called out. "I need your help to reach Ruby. Do you hear me? Ruby ... no, *Rowan* needs your help."

The air next to Ruby shimmered, and there Flint stood, as if he had been beside her all along, merely waiting for Trip's call.

With one hand, the phantom figure, surrounded by a slight glow of blue-white light, reached out and brushed the blond hair away from Ruby's temples. "Rowan, love" Flint said, his voice quiet, but perfectly audible to Trip nonetheless. "Come back to me, sweetheart." He glanced at Trip. "Call her."

If Flint thought Trip's pleas could help induce Ruby to return, he was sadly mistaken. Still, Trip was willing to try anything.

"Ruby," he repeated. "We need you to come back to us. Break the connection."

Once again, Flint spoke words that Trip did not hear.

But Ruby's head dropped forward, down onto her chest, and Trip redoubled his calls to her.

Suddenly, the room grew quiet, and Trip realized that the women around the table had also slumped forward, and the otherworldly wind had stopped.

As Trip stood up, Flint's indistinct form shimmered and faded away. Trip was left with only the afterimage of the other man staring at him fixedly.

"I will take care of her," Trip said aloud, even as he disentangled himself from the women's now-loose grips and moved around the table to kneel beside Ruby.

Her eyelids fluttered twice before she managed to open her eyes completely. Trip stood up long enough to pluck the glass of water from the center of the table and press it into her hands. "Drink this. I'll find something stronger later."

Ruby nodded and took a sip, then cleared her throat. "How is everyone?" she asked, glancing around the room.

I don't care, Trip wanted to say, but he bit down on the words, certain that Ruby wouldn't welcome the sentiment. Anyway, the other women were beginning to stir, and seemed none the worse for wear. "They're OK," he said.

"I hate that term," she said, her voice cracking a little.

Trip laughed softly. "I will try to remember that." He paused. "What do you recall from the séance?"

Ruby put one hand to her forehead. "Everything." She rubbed her palm down over her eyes, then sat up straight, her voice taking on a determined tone. "And I know what we have to do now."

CHAPTER TEN

Despite a bone-aching weariness, Ruby forced herself to stand. The young women around the table were blinking and beginning to speak to one another, discussing the ghost they had all seen in their midst.

None of them remembered anything after Flint's manifestation in the room.

Good.

Ruby, on the other hand, had a visceral memory of the demon's possession of her. If she stopped to think of it, she might vomit.

It was better to move, to begin taking the steps that she hoped might lead to the hell-beast's destruction.

Possibly her own annihilation, as well.

Glancing at Trip, she realized that joining Flint in death didn't seem as appealing as it had only a few hours before.

No. Don't consider that, either. Move forward. Do what must be done. Don't think.

"Follow me," she said quietly to Trip, picking up a candle and leading him out of the room. They slipped out of the boardinghouse before anyone could notice to stop them, Ruby stooping to grab her carpet bag from where she had dropped it in the entryway.

"What do you know?" Trip asked, easily matching her stride.

"Wait," she said, frowning and looking around. Then she shrugged. "Never mind. I don't know where it might be safe to discuss." She ducked behind the corner of a nearby house.

"What I know is that this is definitely the demon. Flint confirmed that much." She opened her carpet bag and began getting ready for the battle she knew was coming. She'd had months to reconsider her actions in the church in New Mexico. This time, she had everything she needed. She was prepared.

Trip blinked when he saw her unfastening her skirt. Ruby knew it was ungentlemanly of him to stare, but she found she didn't care. In fact, she held his gaze with her own as she allowed her skirt and crinoline to puddle to the ground, revealing the Levi's she wore beneath.

Trip's eyes glinted in appreciation. "I thought the gun belt an excellent fashion choice," he said. "It has nothing on this."

"It's practical," Ruby said.

"And lovely."

With a slight smile, she rolled the skirt and placed it in the carpet bag, pulling out her black vest to wear over her shirt. The weapons inside the garment, mostly knives, clinked as she shrugged into it.

She re-settled her gun belt on her hips. "I'm ready."

"Where are we going?" Trip asked.

"Main Street."

Once again, he followed her as she strode out, making her way through the darkened streets.

"The bank and the church are both public buildings, both on Main Street," Ruby said. "They're the only two places we are certain have been attacked by these so-called poltergeists—by the demon, posing as some German-styled ghost. What else do these buildings have in common?"

As they emerged onto Main Street, the town's few streetlamps offered scant illumination.

But it was enough to see what she meant.

"They're both being faced with rocks," Trip said.

"Exactly," Ruby replied. "Why are these buildings being faced with the quarried stones?"

Trip's brow furrowed in thought. "I hadn't considered it. I assume they will last longer that way. Not need for painting or much other maintenance."

"No. I mean, why construct the buildings from wood at all? Those rocks are everywhere. Wood is much less abundant. Why not use the stones to build with from the beginning?"

Trip frowned. "You're right."

"When the demon had me in its grip it said it had been 'part of this earth for all time.' I believe the demon is somehow tied to the stones the townspeople are using. They didn't build with it from the beginning because somehow, the demon stopped them."

"Now that they're using it to face their buildings..." Trip said.

"...the demon is fighting back," Ruby finished his sentence for him.

Trip glanced down, where tiny pebbles littered the ground beneath their feet, and his face fell. "How can we possibly exorcise the demon from the earth itself?"

"It also said that it was 'but a fraction of the land.' I think that was literal, Trip. It is a piece of this larger whole. Connected to it. All we have to do...."

"...is remove it from any single part." Now Trip was the one finishing her sentences.

"Exactly." Ruby gestured at the pile of rocks waiting in front of the bank for workers to finish the work they had begun. "And we have a perfect part waiting for us, right here."

Without warning, Trip swooped her up in his arms and spun around. "You are brilliant."

She hit him on one shoulder. "Put me down, Flint." Her voice echoed with laughter, but as soon as the words were out of her mouth, she froze, her eyes wide. "Oh, no. Trip. I am sorry."

He shook his head, letting her slide down his body until her boots touched the ground, still holding her close. "It's OK, Ruby. I understand." Slowly, he pressed his lips to hers, giving her ample time to pull away.

She didn't.

Instead, she returned the pressure of his lips, first tentatively, then with more enthusiasm.

When he finally ended the kiss, they were both breathless.

"Shall we go exorcise some rocks?" he asked.

"Absolutely."

* * *

Trip glanced at the sky, gauging the time until dawn. Hours, he guessed. It wasn't much past midnight. In a perfect world, he and Ruby would be completing this work immediately before sunrise, their exorcism reinforced by the light of the sun.

Then again, in a perfect world, they wouldn't be performing an exorcism at all.

If they survived this, it would a miracle.

He stared at the woman kneeling in front of the pile of stones, pulling exorcism paraphernalia out of a carpet bag, preparing to rid an entire town of the demon haunting it, and thought of the man she had lost, of the gentle way his spirit had reached out to brush her hair from her temple. And he thought of the command that ghost had given Trip to care for her, as if he knew that Ruby and Trip would need one another, and wanted to give it his blessing.

Sometimes, miracles happen.

Ruby paused in laying out her various ritual items. "Trip?" she asked, her voice tentative.

"Yeah?"

"Do you think Flint will ever come back to me again?"

Reaching out his own hand, he smoothed back the tendrils of hair framing her face. "I don't think he'll ever leave," he said softly.

"Good." She took his hand in her own and rested her

cheek against it briefly, then went back to arranging for her ceremony.

When she was finished, she stood and checked over her preparations one last time. Trip recognized some of the elements—a pentagram scratched into the dirt, with elements piled at each point, or in the case of the final one, water soaking the dusty ground, a circle enclosing it all. The smudge stick lay next to an unlit match, ready to be burned when necessary.

"When I pull the demon out of the stones, he's likely to come at us fast and hard," Ruby said. "We'll need to be ready to defend one another."

"Will you need to be able to move around to complete the ceremony?" Trip asked.

"No."

"Then I suggest we prepare now." He turned his back to hers, readying himself to cover one side of the street.

Ruby pressed her back against Trip's. "What kind of ammunition do you have?" she asked.

"Silver. Tremayne insisted on it when I was assigned out here."

"Good. It's one of the few things that seems to repel the demonic forces."

He grinned as he looked over his shoulder at her. "Isn't it a little late to be asking that?"

Ruby's laugh stemmed as much from nerves as amusement, Trip suspected. "Probably. I only thought of it this moment."

"Well, I'm good. You ready?"

Her back heaved against his once as she breathed in. "Let's go."

Once again, as when he first came to town—only the morning before, though it seemed much longer ago—and again during the séance, Ruby's low, alto voice formed a humming undercurrent to the power that began to swirl around them. This time, though, Trip could feel the vibration of her back against his as she spoke.

This is how it should be.

The two of them, standing together, fighting against whatever evil forces might attempt to take them down.

Even as the misty form of the demon rose up into the air in front of him, Trip knew with a certainty he felt through his whole being, that as long as they worked together, they would defeat it.

* * *

Ruby's exhaustion played against her as she used all her strength to pull the demon out of the rocks in the pile in front of the bank, and she almost lost her grip on the beast when Mr. Schmidt, the bank manager, came scuttling around the corner.

"Get back," she ordered, and the round man froze, his face a mask of sheer horror as he saw the demonic form— vaguely human, but covered with scales and a visage so frightening that she didn't wonder at the man's response.

He paled even further, if that was indeed possible, and disappeared back the way he came.

I guess that answers the question of whether Mr. Schmidt contacted the Tremayne PSI Agency as the demon's accomplice or pawn.

To anyone on the outside, it would look as if the demon merely hovered in the air above them as Ruby and Trip stood back-to-back. But Ruby trembled with the effort of holding it outside the stones, pulling it through the earth from the quarry where it drew its own power, and forcing it into corporeal form.

"Tell me when to shoot," Trip had said grimly, then linked arms with Ruby and dug his heels into the earth, keeping them steady.

The momentary distraction of Mr. Schmidt allowed the demon to gain traction, pulling at Ruby and slipping back into the stones.

"No," Ruby gritted out, joining her aura to Trip's and allowing the flaring light to fuel her determination.

The additional power flooded through her, and she poured it into her intentions, shoving it through the pentagram and the elements. As the demon took solid form, settling on the ground, the wind around them picked up, swirling as it had the morning before.

"Smudge-stick," she shouted over her shoulder to Trip, who reacted as if they had rehearsed it. Unhooking one arm, he waited for her to grab the smudge-stick and match from the ground, then swung her around, as if finishing a do-si-do, ending with Ruby huddled against his chest as he held a gun on the demon.

It took three tries to light the sage bundle without letting the demon loose from her confining will, but she managed it, and when she was ready, Trip spun her around, again without ever letting go, to face the monster, now fully embodied. "I have to go all the way around it," she shouted.

Trip simply picked her up, his own muscles straining against the force of the demonic winds attempting to hold them back. Ruby shook even more than before with the effort of sprinkling salt and smudging the circle.

When they finished, sweat drenched both Ruby and Trip, but she knew they were almost done. The beast stood trapped in the circle, the pentagram keeping it from sending out its own magic. A shimmering dome, like a crystal bowl turned upside down, held the monstrous creature at bay.

"Now," Ruby said, her voice threaded with exhaustion. "Shoot it now."

"Will the bullets cause the barrier to collapse?" he asked worriedly.

"No." She kept one arm looped through his, but gave up the other to allow him to aim.

Inside the trap, the demon roared and screamed dire threats, clawing at the invisible walls holding it in.

Trip took aim, and Ruby worked to remain motionless, to avoid jarring his arm as he pulled the trigger.

The bubble of power shimmered when the silver

bullets pierced it, wobbling as if it might pop, but remained upright. With an agonized screech, the demon grasped its abdomen. Despite its inhuman countenance, every line of its face betrayed its shock at being wounded.

"There, you son of a bitch," Ruby whispered. The demon's head whipped around toward her, and she realized it could hear her.

Good.

She had some things to say.

"You took the most precious thing I had and destroyed it. I can't imagine you value anything more than your own hide. So now I'm making sure you lose. You hear that, you bastard? *You lose.*"

Trip had stopped shooting as she spoke, allowing her time to say her piece, as if he understood her need for words.

"I'm done," she said. "Kill it."

Trip's silver bullets finished the job, the demon collapsing into a pile inside the containment circle. As the last of its life-force bled out onto the ground, the incandescent bubble containing it disappeared.

Ruby watched it die, then sent her paranormal senses questing through the town.

Nothing.

She was sure of it.

The townspeople of Rittersburg might someday have an actual poltergeist to deal with. But for now, they were free of all supernatural forces.

She glanced up at Trip. His face was pale and drawn, but satisfied, and she knew she couldn't have done it without him.

He returned her gaze, and a slight smile crossed his face. "I don't know about you, but I could use some sleep," Trip said, threading his fingers through hers and tugging her toward Mrs. Baumgartner's.

"OK," Ruby said, laughing at his open-mouthed outrage at her use of the term. "But we sleep in our own beds."

She paused, glancing at him. "For now."

"For now," he agreed. "But only because I am exhausted."

She glanced heavenward. *And because I am not yet ready, Flint. But I will be. Eventually.*

For the first time since walking away from that church in New Mexico, Ruby actually felt alive.

* * *

As she finally drifted to sleep in the bed she was using for the first time in the Gasthof, Ruby imagined Flint stroking the hair back from her face, as he used to do. Then she was half-dreaming, half-remembering his shade as it stood next to her during the séance the night before.

"Rowan," he said, his blue-gray eyes kind as he reached out, not quite touching her. "I want you to be happy. I mean that. More than anything, I want you to be happy." His gaze flicked toward Trip, who was watching the scene play out before him with his usual calculating stare hidden beneath a lazy half-smile. "Let yourself be loved, sweetheart," Flint continued. "Allow someone else to look out for you, watch over you."

Ruby's shoulders heaved, and the part of her mind that knew this was only a memory felt her body twitch. But she didn't wake. The dream played itself out to its end, as if reminding her of her promise.

"I will," she said.

Flint turned to Trip and said something she hadn't heard during the actual séance—now, however, the sound carried with perfect clarity. "You will care for her," Flint announced, his words to the other man bearing the weight of a directive from the Great Beyond. "Protect her."

Trip nodded solemnly.

Trip doesn't understand that he's now compelled by two competing mystical bindings. One to part ways with me when this case ends, the other to protect me. Indefinitely.

Their conflicting constraints would tear him apart.

And only Ruby could release him from one of them.

For that matter, she realized, Flint had placed her under an obligation of her own—to allow herself to be cared for. Then he had connected it, at least tangentially, to the oath he had extracted from Trip.

Damn you, Flint. You sneaky son of a bitch. Alone in her mind, she could curse and call him all the names she wanted, be as unladylike as she had sometimes been with him.

She almost heard the echo of his laughter, pleased with himself and his machinations.

It's what you need, my love, she heard him say.

This time, when she felt the brush of his fingers against her temple, she drifted into a true sleep—where she dreamed of Trip, standing back to back with her, facing anything that might come their way.

* * *

Afternoon sun streaming through his window woke Trip the next day. He rolled over and groaned, aching and sore all over.

If he really intended to find a way to follow Ruby when she left town, he would need to work on developing his demon-fighting muscles.

Assuming there were any more demons out there to be fought.

Maybe next time we'll get some actual poltergeists.

Or how about a regular old ghost or two? A simple haunting would seem almost pleasant after the last twenty-four hours.

Keep dreaming, Austin.

Somehow, he knew that, although it might often be pleasant, life with Ruby would never be simple.

He dragged himself up to a sitting position as he considered that last thought. Was he seriously planning to try to build a life with this woman after only one day?

I am.

For one thing, he had promised Flint's ghost that he would care for Ruby. That promise held the force of a vow.

More important, though, Trip realized, was the fact that he simply wanted to be with her. She was strong and resourceful and resilient, and from what he had seen of her interactions with Flint's shade, she held a deep reservoir of emotion.

The kind that could water a desert, if she let it.

Trip might not be the man to help her tap into that pool, but he would sure like to try.

A tap at his door interrupted his musings. "Just a minute," he called. He dragged himself out of bed, put on his pants, and made his way to the door. Somehow, he was unsurprised to find Ruby standing outside, a steaming mug in her hand.

"Good morning," she said. "Or rather, afternoon. Here. Drink this. It will make you feel better." Handing the hot drink to him, she swept past him into the room, glancing around appraisingly.

The bitter taste of the tea was barely concealed by the honey that sweetened it. "This is horrible," he said, making a face between sips. "What is it?"

"Witches' brew," she replied distractedly as she pulled open the doors of the armoire. Finding it empty, she closed the doors again and turned to face Trip. When she discovered him staring down into his cup in feigned horror, she shook her head, even as she laughed. "Don't be ridiculous. It's willow bark tea, with a few other herbal ingredients. If you will simply drink it, you should be ready to ride in an hour or so."

He took a long drink, holding his breath. "Ready to ride in an hour?" he said, working to keep his tone as mild as possible.

"Yes." Ruby held her hands out to her sides, palms up. "Our horses are almost ready. Where are your saddle bags?"

"Under the bed." He gestured with the cup before tilting it back to drain it. Grimacing, he set it aside on the washstand.

"Ah, there." Ruby was already dragging the saddlebags out from where he had stashed them. With a slight grunt, she heaved them up onto the mattress.

Recognizing her almost frenzied activity as a mask for worry, Trip stepped forward to intervene as she began to open one of the saddlebags, and placed his hand over hers to still it. "I can pack for myself, Ruby."

She froze, then tilted her head far enough to look at him from under her lashes. Neither said anything at all for a long, quiet moment.

Then she slowly turned her hand palm-up and laced her fingers through his. She closed her eyes, and another surge of power rushed through him. Unlike the others, though, this one didn't hurt.

It did leave him slightly dizzy—or maybe that was the tea.

Or perhaps is was simply Ruby's touch.

Whatever it was, it put a smile on his face.

"You don't have to... ." Ruby's voice trailed off.

"Don't have to what?"

She closed her eyes, took a breath, and stood up straight to look him in the eye—but she didn't let go of his hand.

That's a good sign.

"I have been to the telegram office this morning," she said, her gaze almost as intense as it had been when she had confessed to burning down the church in New Mexico.

"Oh, yeah?"

"The Tremayne Agency will be wiring our pay to San Antonio."

"What's in San Antonio?" he asked.

"Our next case."

Trip didn't know if Ruby was even aware that she was holding her breath. Part of him wanted to tease her a little, make her wait for his confirmation of her unspoken request.

The rest of him wanted to pick her up and spin her around in the air before kissing her soundly. Again.

But either response would be wrong.

"Our case?" he repeated.

Her voice dropped. "If you're willing to partner with me, that is."

A slow smile spread across his face, and in a moment, it was matched by Ruby's grin. Trip picked up their clasped hands, turned them over, and dropped a light kiss on the back of her wrist.

"What are we looking at when we get there?" he asked, letting go of Ruby and pulling open the straps of the saddlebag.

Ruby handed him a shirt from where it hung on the slat-back rocker in the corner of the room. "It looks to be interesting—apparently there's some kind of water-creature haunting a bridge across the river there. Nat Tremayne seems to think it might be a troll."

Trip's heart grew lighter as he listened to Ruby outline what she knew about trolls.

Oh, yes. It looks to be interesting, indeed.

DID YOU LIKE WILD WILD GHOST?

Please consider leaving an honest review on Amazon and Goodreads. Reviews help others find books and it helps the authors out tremendously. Thank you in advance.

ABOUT THE AUTHOR

Margo Bond Collins is addicted to coffee and SF/F television, especially *Supernatural* (maybe because of those Winchesters). She writes contemporary and paranormal romance, urban fantasy, and paranormal mystery. She lives in Texas with her daughter and several spoiled pets. Although she teaches college-level English courses online, writing fiction is her first love. She enjoys reading romance and paranormal fiction of any genre and spends most of her free time daydreaming about heroes, cowboys, vampires, ghosts, werewolves, and the women who love (and sometimes fight) them.

You can learn more about her at www.MargoBondCollins.net and follow her on all the usual social media outlets.

SUBSCRIBE TO MARGO'S NEWSLETTER
For updates about Margo's publications, news about her new releases, great book deals. free fiction, and other goodies, be sure to sign up for Margo's general newsletter at eepurl.com/caUeyr or scan this QR Code:

JOIN THE VAMPIRARCHY, MARGO'S STREET TEAM
Want to hang out with the author, win book prizes, see the covers first, and support Margo's books on social media? Join The Vampirarchy, Margo's street team on Facebook at www.facebook.com/groups/vampirarchy or scan this QR Code: